HUNTER I

ADVENTURES IN LOVE, LIFE AND LARCENY

By William Serle

Hunter I

First in the trilogy,
Hunter I, Hunter II,* and *Hunter III

Published by William Serle
billserle.com

ISBN 978-0615791340

Also by William Serle

- *Stealing Ali* – Written with Daisy Serle
- *Bill's Journey* – A memoir
- *Hunter I* – Adventures in love, life and larceny
- *Hunter II* – A tale of love and crime
- *Hunter III* – Paul in the year 2055 and beyond

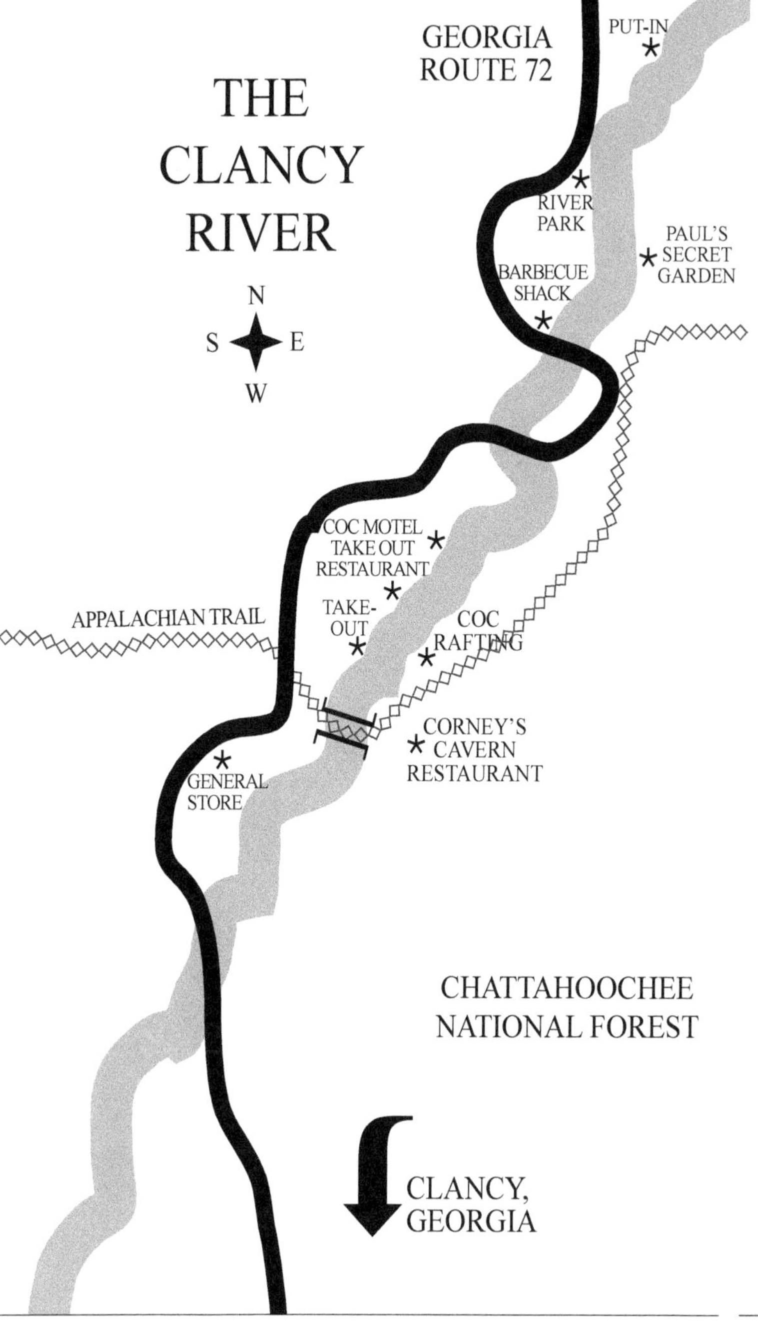
THE CLANCY RIVER
GEORGIA ROUTE 72
PUT-IN
N
S
E
W
RIVER PARK
PAUL'S SECRET GARDEN
BARBECUE SHACK
COC MOTEL
TAKE OUT RESTAURANT
APPALACHIAN TRAIL
TAKE-OUT
COC RAFTING
CORNEY'S CAVERN RESTAURANT
GENERAL STORE
CHATTAHOOCHEE NATIONAL FOREST
CLANCY, GEORGIA

For the family I've loved forever

I want to thank folks who helped me by reading the story for proofing, editing and loving support.
Daisy Serle, Jeff Serle, Diana Huntress
and Sandy Selders.
The good parts are yours – the blunders are mine.

TABLE OF CONTENTS

PART 4

PART 1

THURSDAY, AUGUST 22, 1991

Paul leaned against the chain link fence and watched Debby approach. She seemed to be looking right at him. He was puzzled by her eye contact since she had pretty much ignored his existence since the start of Huntsville P.S. 21's fall term. He noticed everything about her. Their too-short lunch break was almost over on this sunny Thursday.

Debby Malone was tall for a 13 year-old girl and very well developed. Her red hair was pulled back into a ponytail that bounced with every bold step. She seemed to be marching toward him. Her red satin shirt, well-filled blue jeans and matching red sandals gave her costume a finished, thought-out look. Paul considered her the hottest girl in his history class.

He wasn't actually thinking at this moment, though. He was nearing girl-panic but tried to mask it by deliberately keeping his face blank. He stood away from the fence as she came to a halt.

“Hi Debby.” Their noses were just 2 feet apart, and she had him nailed with her blue eyes.

“Paul. What did you mean when you said that in class?”

“What? Do you mean about the Irish immigrants to New York being luckier than the Poles?”

“Yeah,” she almost snarled. “My grandpa was Irish and he had a terrible time. He got into trouble and ran away to Alabama when he was 21. That’s how my family got here and I think it was very hard. I’m going to be the first high school graduate in my family if I can hold on for 4 more years.”

“Well I didn’t mean anything. I just figured that they had it easier since they already spoke English and could blend in better. Um…”

She interrupted him by saying, archly, “I guess you’re Polish. Huh.”

He began to answer but the school bell jangled the end of the lunch period. She spun around and marched away before he could decide how to answer. Debby didn’t say goodbye or even give him a head-bob.

Paul didn’t know where his family came from. He guessed they were English and had arrived a long time ago. He decided to ask his brother Mitch, after school or, maybe, his parents at dinner.

“Uh. See ya,” he called out lightly. He was glad that the day was half over and gave no further thought to Debby Malone. His mind was busy with after-school plans.

Paul Hunter was not the best student at P.S. 21. He got good grades by listening in class but he hated homework, except for English literature. He would read anything that came his way but he preferred novels. His older brother was reading Moby Dick in high school now. Paul was proud that he'd already read it by taking it out of the library.

Well above average height, Paul had erect posture and broad shoulders. On the thin side now, he would gain bulk and become a formidable man in a few years. His hair was dark and his eyes were a light hazel like his brother's.

For no particular reason the boys never got involved in school athletics. They could have developed sports skills but their parents did not push them in that direction.

They had moved to Huntsville early in 1989 when Paul was just 10 years old. Mitch was 14 then and, since school was in recess, they'd formed a tight bond. Strange to say, they never fought other than wrestling and horseplay for fun. They were best friends. Paul, a little shy, was happy to get his older brother's attention.

Mitch tried out for the swim team as a high school freshman but the coaches were not impressed enough to put him on the team. There were boys who had been honing their competitive skills for years in area swimming clubs.

The brothers were not under the benign influence of organized athletic competition. Work, boy adventures, and home life were the center of their first years in Huntsville.

Paul was anxious to finish the school day. The family was making plans to go camping and canoeing on the banks of the Tennessee River on Labor Day weekend in 2 weeks. He and Mitch had a lot to do to get their tent and camping gear together. He hoped they could go to buy paddles on Saturday. He wanted a cool wooden one so that he could say, “no thanks,” when the canoe rental guy told him to choose a plastic one. They had their own tents but not boats.

Money was not a problem. He and Mitch had plenty since they’d been hard at work for several years on a number of projects. Most of them were legal but a few were not. The more lucrative jobs were often a little evil. So far they’d never been caught.

Paul walked home since it was less than a mile away. Debby, who lived in the same direction, caught up with him. She seemed a little out of breath. They were approaching her dark red brick apartment building. His house was a few blocks further away from school.

“Hey, Paul.”

“Hey, Debbie.”

“Say, Paul. I. I-um-…wanted to ask you.” She looked a little troubled.

“Paul. Have you ever had a yen?”

“What do you mean?”

“You know.” She was looking at him. Her head was lowered and her shoulders were a little slumped. “Like to do something you shouldn’t?”

“Well. I guess. But what do y…” He was interrupted by a sudden shout.

“DEBBY!” Her mother was shouting from the window of Debbie’s apartment. “HURRY UP, DEBBY! WE’RE WAITING FOR YOU.”

"Paul," Debby straightened up and looked him in the eye. Her lids were half closed and she hesitated as if she was thinking something over. "Paul. Come to my house tonight at about eight-thirty. Don't ring the bell. Just climb that tree there. There." She pointed to a towering oak growing behind her apartment, "...and wait for me. Be quiet."

She turned and ran around the corner and into the apartment. Her mother was holding the front door open. "Sorry, Deb. Aunt Betty is waiting for us and we have got to go. Put your books in your room and let's get it on."

Paul sauntered home, deep in thought, anxious to talk to Mitch.

Paul's parents, Samantha and Michael Hunter, and his 16-year old brother Mitch were close-knit. They did not have other family nearby and were happy in each other's company.

Paul, a normal 12-year-old pre-teen, was past puberty. He had learned the facts of life some years earlier, thanks to his older brother's research and experience. Neither Mom nor Dad had broached the subject of sex with him or with Mitch for that matter. They were content to believe that their boys would figure things out for themselves or ask if they had questions.

The boys huddled after supper. "Mitch. This girl Debby wants me to climb the tree outside her window tonight. Do you think I should go?"

"I dunno. What'd she say?" Mitch was very interested in this report from his little brother.

Paul recounted his conversations with Debby. Mitch was excited. "Paul. You gotta go and I'll go with you, but you have to do something for me later. Okay?"

“What Mitch?”

“Nothing important. Just some fun I want to have at Eddie’s house a little later.”

“Mom. We’re going to see Eddie. Okay? We’ll be back in a little while.” It was just after eight o'clock and dinner was finished. Pot roast.

“Okay boys. Take care to get back before bedtime. Tomorrow’s a school day.”

The door slammed behind them and Mitch said, “Paul. Wait a minute. There’s something I got to get.” He disappeared into the driveway that ran next to the house. Paul patiently waited on the dark street.

When he reappeared, Mitch was carrying a little paper sack.

“What’s that?” said Paul.

“Well, listen here bro. This is a sack of dog shit that I’m going to leave on Pete Jones’ front porch. I’m going to set it on fire and run like hell. You come with me and be my lookout. I don’t want anybody to see it.”

Paul had been curious about the sudden rank aroma that seemed to emanate from Mitch, “What the Hell, Mitch. What did Eddie do to you? He probably won’t answer the door anyways. His mom or dad will have to deal with it.”

“Naw. They’re going to a meeting tonight. I just want to pay him back for some dog shit he left in my locker at school. Everybody made fun of me because my books stank and I didn’t know why. He laughed his ass off and I have to get even. Okay?

“Okay. But we do Debby’s tree first. Okay?”

“Okay.”

The street by Debby's apartment was quiet and the boys were hidden in the leaves of the tree opposite the second story windows. There was a play of lights inside the apartment as lights turned off and on. Peoples' shadows shifted inside.

A light went on in a downstairs window and they saw Mr. Malone sit at a window-side table, curtains gently blowing as the evening air stirred. The leaves rustled, too. Mr. Malone placed a briefcase on the table and began rummaging through it as the boys saw a second floor room light up.

The shade was up and Debby walked into the room in a light blue bathrobe. She stood in the center of the room and seemed to be staring through the window at them as she began toying with the sash. They practically fell off their branch when she dropped the robe. She was naked except for white panties that kept her bottom covered as well as a bikini bathing suit. She turned away from them but they clearly saw her breasts and then her back as she walked out of the room and closed the door.

Mr. Malone was now the only show and they saw that he was removing cash from his case. He began arranging the bills on the table. He was counting the money and putting the bills into different stacks.

"Holy shit. These are interesting people," Mitch whispered.

Paul didn't answer but squeezed Mitch's shoulder. A short time later the second floor door opened and Debbie walked in again. She still wore her panties but her breasts were again in full view, and she looked better than a woman in a girly magazine to them. Her pink nipples put them in a trance. They couldn't move.

Debby's mom appeared in the doorway as Debby stepped into pajamas and raised her arms to shrug into her pajama top. Her boobs bounced a little. Her mom walked to the shade and lowered it without looking outside.

"Paul," Mitch's whisper was urgent, "Change of plans. I'm going to put the shit on their porch and light it off. When it gets going good, I'm gonna ring the bell and run the other way and make sure that they see my back. Maybe Mr. Malone will chase me. Anyways, don't follow me. Go home the other way. If he gets up to answer the doorbell, grab some of the cash through the window will ya. Be quiet about it and run like hell. I'll see you at home. Okay?"

"Okay, but..."

Mitch was gone in an instant leaving behind a whiff of dog shit. Paul sat still, wondering if the show was over. He was both scared and excited. Visions of Debby's breasts and look of her skin sifted through his boy brain. Another upstairs room lit, but the curtains remained closed. Mr. Malone sat at the table busy with his task.

Paul heard the doorbell and smelled smoke at the same time. Mr. Malone got up and left the picture. Paul climbed quietly to the ground and advanced on the window to see that Mr. Malone had been stacking the bills by denomination. There were little piles of hundreds and fifties and larger stacks of twenty-dollar bills and smaller denominations.

Paul heard a loud "God dammit!" from the front of the house as he reached in and took the larger bills off the table. The ones, tens and fives he scattered off the table toward the windowsill to make it look like a gust of wind might have moved things. As he turned to run, he saw one more thing on the table – a large, black revolver. The sight of the pistol shook him and he began running for home, stuffing the bills in his pocket.

Mitch looked up and down the street. It was dark except for the occasional porch lamp. He held the bag and a small box of wooden matches in one hand and used the banister to steady himself. He steeled himself and lit the bag bottom and top in three places. The sack was small but well packed with droppings. He waited as long as he dared then rang the bell twice before running.

Mitch paused in the shadow of a large tree trunk directly across the street and was rewarded by the sight of Mr. Malone standing over the paper bag. He raised his slippered foot to stomp out the little fire and the bag exploded into a stinking, smoldering mess that splattered on his legs and over the porch.

"God dammit!" He hopped around trying to figure out where to put his other foot and, in a moment, figured out what had happened. He saw Mitch's figure in the deep shadows, and began running. Malone thought that he saw two boys and ran toward them. "God damned kids!

Mitch whirled around and took off at a run. Malone was fast and began to close the distance. Mitch heard his pursuer's footfalls, his heavy breathing and a muttered, "I'll see which one of youse bastards can run the fastest." The old guy was incredibly fast. That muttered threat inspired Mitch to shift into high gear and he got well ahead of the cursing and growling man.

Malone lost a slipper and hobbled to a halt. "I'll gettcha you bastard!" he yelled. But Mitch was around the corner and took a roundabout path home in case the old man spotted him again.

The excitement was over. Home, showered, and dressed for bed, the boys finally had time to put their heads together. Mitch whispered, "$770.00. Holy mackerel, Paul. Hell of a night, eh?"

"Mitch. What are we gonna do with the money. If Mom or Dad finds out about this, there'll be hell to pay. We godda think of something. And, oh, I forgot to tell you, Mr. Malone had a gun on the table. A big one, like in the movie *Dirty Harry*. You think he might be into something illegal with all that cash? Drugs?"

"I dunno. Sounds like it. I hope Debby keeps her mouth shut about you. Us. She probably doesn't know about me but she could figure it out."

After a brief pause, Mitch said, "You know, we already had about a hundred dollars in the jar from the newspaper box break-ins we did. Now it's a lot of money and we have got to find a way of using it; like laundering it so that we can spend it without Mom and Dad getting onto us, and I have an idea."

Paul nodded, "Tell me. Quick. I'm getting sleepy."

"Okay. So we go over to Cantor's Cash And Carry Restaurant Supply Company and get some gear for selling lemonade at the ball games at the park. We don't have to make a lot of money – we just have got to say that we're making money."

"Sounds good. It sounds like fun. We'll get on it tomorrow afternoon. Okay. I want to get that paddle."

“Okay. Good night.”

Mitch left. Closing the door. Paul snuggled under the covers squeezing his erect penis. He wanted to think about the canoe paddle but Debbie’s face was in his reverie. They were nose to nose and he wanted to kiss her. And touch her…

FRIDAY, AUGUST 23, 1991

"Mom. You know I want to buy a canoe paddle at the outfitters store for our camping trip?"

"Yes Paul, and I already told you yes, but you'd have to earn the money yourself and I know that you don't have enough."

"Me and Mitch…"

"Mitch and I," she corrected him, archly, but with love in her face.

"I mean Mitch and I have an idea. I have enough cash, and Mitch will help me, to buy some stuff at Cantor's. We think we can sell lemonade at the ball games if we have a carrying rack that will hold a buncha cups."

"Yes, but you guys will have to do it on your own. You know how busy Dad is right now and I'm tied up getting ready to take off for our vacation trip."

"Thanks Ma. I knew you'd say yes.

Paul left the house for school on time, keeping his eyes open for Debby. He was terrified of facing her for two reasons. The least of the two was her father's gun. The other was that he wanted to see her naked again; so bad that it made his throat constrict.

Debby was not in history class. He looked for her in the schoolyard and on the way home to meet Mitch for their shopping expedition to the Cash and Carry. No sign of her on the street and he was leery of walking by her apartment building.

SATURDAY, AUGUST 24, 1991

The boys had an impressive kit gathered for their business venture. They intended to haul the family ice chest, a few gallons of mixed lemonade and a 20-cup caddy with shoulder straps in Dad's big wheelbarrow. They had a carton of plastic cups, straws, and lids. They planned to pick up a supply of ice at a convenient gas station and obtain more water for their jugs with a short garden hose from the tap they'd spotted at the ball field.

There was a carton of instant-lemonade powder packets that made a gallon each. They had pliers to turn the water on since they'd noticed that there was no handle at the park's spigot. They were set to sell hundreds of cups at 50 cents each. They had rolls of quarters and 50 one-dollar bills at the ready to make change. Mitch would hawk their wares and Paul would mix more product or make an ice run if necessary.

"Paul. Remember that there probably are rules against doing this. So we gotta work fast. I figure if we get busted they'll just tell us to leave and we can come back when they aren't looking."

"Okay Mitch."

The big lie would be that they didn't care too much if sales were lousy or if they got chased. "Remember kid," Mitch said with a wink, "we're just laundering money like on TV. We'll tell Mom and Dad that we made $125.00 so's we can get a pair of those swell wooden paddles."

The park was crowded with junior league baseball fans. It was hot and the work was brutal. The facility had multiple ball fields. The area they worked had 4 fields with 8 bleachers arranged around a bathroom and concession stand. The concession stand sold drinks but no one in an official capacity took notice of them. There was a good crowd – mostly parents and siblings rooting for family members.

The boys sold 220 glasses of lemonade at 50¢ each in 3 hours when they ran out of ice and the crowds began to thin. They cleared $14.00 after deducting all costs including $50.00 for the strapped carriers. Next time the carriers, cups, lids, straws and mix would be already on hand and not have to be bought. Their net would shoot up.

"And ya know Paul. We could make more if we were more efficient. We'll have to figure out how to get us both in the stands at the same time instead of you just filling cups with ice and juice," Mitch grinned as Paul wheeled the barrow down the street.

"Yeah Mitch. We'll start with more ice too next time. And we'll take the ice pick."

“And tomorrow we’ll get our paddles. We can take the bus if we can’t get Mom or Dad to take us. Let’s say we made $140.00 today. It would take an audit of our stuff to prove otherwise, and no one’s going to do that.”

SUNDAY AUGUST 25, 1991

The Hunter family sat at the dinner table. With no school and, usually, no work on Sunday, they always tried to gather for the supper meal, conversation and, TV together after cleanup. The sweet aroma of roasted chicken was in the air.

"Well boys, Mom told me you raked in some good money at the ball game. It's a shame you spent it on the paddles, but I guess they'll last for years. Good job! Sorry I was too busy to help."

Michael Hunter was a builder. He held a general contractor license in Alabama but, when he didn't have a project of his own, he worked as a supervisor for others. Sometimes, if he needed to, he could work as a carpenter. He made a good living.

“Thanks Dad,” Mitch nodded. “We’re going to keep on selling the juice through the football season. We’ll do even better now that we’ve got our gear paid for.” Both boys were beaming. It was good to be a Hunter.

Mom worked too. She was a licensed financial advisor. She now worked on a fee basis but had started in insurance sales. She and her husband of 19 years were fairly prosperous now but, at her urging, they always saved for a rainy day. They were comfortable and even thinking of how to get the kids through college. Since the boys were not great scholars they foresaw community college and, if that worked out, a university education.

“I’ve been busy too guys,” she announced. “But you showed real get up and go there. I’m glad you got your paddles. We’ll have a good time camping.

“Say Mike,” she turned to her husband. “My friend Patsy who owns the apartment building and I had coffee today. Guess what?”

The three turned toward her expectantly.

“She had the apartment rented to a family named Malone and they left town leaving all their stuff in the apartment. They left her a note saying to go ahead and re-let the place and please feel free to use or dispose of their furniture. They just took their clothing and the TV. The note said they had to leave the area due to an emergency.

The boys eyed each other. In a nano-second they warned each other to be careful. Paul began to feel guilty about the affair. There were consequences he hadn’t intended,

“Paul. Didn’t you go to school with the daughter? What’s her name?”

"Yes Mom. Her name's Debby. She was in my history class.

"By the way. We had a sort of argument the other day. She said her grandparents were Irish and I didn't know when the Hunters or your family came to America or where they were from.

"So Mom, what are we anyway? I mean English, Polish or what?"

The camping trip was brilliant. The Hunters felt close in spirit as well as physically. The family tent was big enough for four sleeping rolls and not much else. There was a big awning attached to the front and they faced it right to the water of Lake Surprise.

The rented canoes were pulled up on the beach at their doorstep. There was a fire pit, an iron charcoal barbecue, and a picnic table in their campsite. Shower and toilet facilities, with hot water were nearby. Each campsite was slightly separated from neighbors by trees and brush but they got to know their neighbors and felt part of a friendly community.

Three days of paddling, hiking, camp cooking, taking all their meals together and enjoying fine fall weather relaxed the Hunters. The boys liked their new paddles and, since no motorboats were permitted, the atmosphere was serene. The lake was large enough for exploration and fishing. They swam from their campsite and a large public beach.

FRIDAY, SEPTEMBER 25, 1992

Fall was incredible. The boys were busy with school and their lemonade-vending/money-laundering scheme.

Paul continued to feel guilty about snatching the money from Debby's father and even more guilty about her disappearance from the neighborhood and school. He had no way of knowing whether he was responsible but he suspected that his role had helped no one.

Mitch was more stoic about the matter. "Forget about it Paul. People move all the time and you can never know if that money had anything to do with it. He may have been getting it together as a part of his moving plan. Lots of people have guns."

For Mitch, the sudden appearance of Molly Kravitz became the focus of his attention. She was a year older than him but they were in some of the same classes at school. They became friendly when he discovered that she worked in the neighborhood.

Molly worked part time at the corner Bohacks Grocery store until it closed at 8 PM. Mitch was there to meet her almost every night and Paul sometimes tagged along.

The meets with Molly were not dates. They were more like hanging out. Usually there was a walk to Molly's house and a peck goodnight so she could get her dinner and do her homework. Once in a while they'd hang out for a while, right by Bohacks – Paul would chat with Molly for a moment and then give the couple a little space so that they could smooch in relative privacy in the shadows in the alley.

Paul noticed that there was once a doorway in the brick wall while he was waiting for Mitch and Molly. It was now boarded up and painted brick red; the same shade as the building itself.

He knew the store well and realized that there were shelves of canned vegetables on the other side of the boarded-up door. He pressed his eye up to a knothole. To Paul's surprise he had a clear view of Larry, the owner, emptying the cash register into a little metal box and then putting the box behind the Post cereal boxes behind the counter. He watched for a moment longer and the lights went out.

As Larry locked the store and walked away, Molly and Mitch said goodbye. She walked toward home and the boys walked together toward their house.

"Guess what Mitch?"

"What."

"I know where Larry leaves the store's cash overnight." Paul said importantly.

"Where? How do you know?"

Paul explained what he saw. "And those boards are just nailed. Nothing fancy. I was thinking when I looked at them that someone could just pry some of those boards out and crawl in, right over the peas and corn, and be back outside of the store in less than a minute.

"And, if it was me, I'd do it right away tonight. Dad's pry bar and hammer are on the basement workbench. If I was to do it tonight, after Mom and Dad went to bed, I'd be back home in less than 15 minutes." Paul was a little wrought up and began breathing hard as he looked at Mitch striding next to him.

"Wow little brother. You're becoming a badass. Why do you want to do it?"

"I don't know," Paul said slowly. "I know we don't need the money now but we'll think of something. We're almost done laundering the Malone money. We could keep it going and we're actually making money on the lemonade. We could get rich.

"What do you think? Should I do it?"

"It's tempting. I don't like Larry very much. He's real bossy around Molly and he watches me like a hawk when I'm in the store. As if I'd actually steal a can of beans.

"If you want to do it, I'll go with you. Stay dressed when you get in bed. We'll need to be really quiet getting out and getting back home. We can get the tools off the bench before bed, but we can't put them away until tomorrow morning."

Paul was suddenly a little scared but he didn't want to look like a chicken. Besides, it was his idea.

SATURDAY, SEPTEMBER 26, 1992 – 1 AM

The board gave a loud squeal as Mitch pried it loose.

"Shh." Paul quavered. "Do it slow."

Mitch growled, "Shut up you little shit. I'm doing it as quiet as I can." He began work on the second board and it was quieter. Two boards were enough. Even though the planks were still attached at one end, there was enough room for Paul to scoot through. Cans fell to the floor but he ignored them. He ran around the counter, found the box, and soon handed it through the opening to Mitch.

The boys replaced the boards by hand pressing the nails back into their original holes. The nails were not too warped from the prying. Mitch tapped them back into place with the rubber end of the hammer handle. The thumps were well-muffled.

The streets were empty and they were back in their beds without incident. Neither boy slept very well. They would count their haul later.

Two weeks later the news in the neighborhood was that Bohacks was closing. Word was that the new Publix had stolen too many customers. Bohacks was a very convenient store for those in the neighborhood but it could not keep up with modern supermarket innovations and prices.

DECEMBER 31, 1992

Paul was having a happy day. It was his 14th birthday and his parents were celebrating with a few friends at home and Paul was very much a part of the party. He would get presents, attention, and a birthday cake. The only fly in the ointment was that Mitch would not be there.

"Sorry little brother. It's party night and I'm going to a class party with Molly. I'll be thinking about ya though. Happy birthday old buddy."

Mitch was able to buy a 1985 F150 pickup truck when he got his driver's license in the spring. It was a sharp looking rig with a cool fiberglass tonneau cover. Mitch had the $1,000.00 down payment and needed his parents to finance the balance. Having his own set of wheels gave him a lot of independence as well as responsibilities.

The boys' days of crime and laundering money were over. They worked weekends for their dad and his business friends on a variety of construction jobs. They sometimes worked as a team but were more independent now that they were older and had their own set of friends. Paul was now a little too young to run with Mitch's crowd.

Paul went to bed happy. He was fourteen now, getting closer to getting his license to drive, feeling prosperous, and in control. He woke while it was still dark. His clock told him it was 3 AM. He walked into the hallway and saw that his mother and father were dressing."

"Hey. What's up?"

"Paul. You can go back to bed. Mitch has had an accident. He's not hurt, but we have to go to the police station to see him."

"Oh my gosh! I want to go with you." Paul whirled around and was pulling on jeans and a tee shirt before they could stop him. In less than a minute the 3 were through the front door and on the way.

The police substation was a grim, utilitarian building. The detective was grim too. "No sir. You cannot see him at this point. He's under arrest and he'll need an attorney. We are holding him in a cell here until morning when the state's attorney will determine what charges to file. We have quite a laundry list of possibilities including felonies. The investigator was adamant. Mitch was his prisoner now more than he was their child and brother.

"Do you have an attorney?"

"Yes sir. May I use your phone?"

It was noon, the first day of 1993, when they left the police station. They, Mom, Dad and Paul, had to leave without Mitch. Attorney Monroe Gelb had done his best but there were several charges including: vehicular homicide, failure to have a vehicle under control, speeding, possession of marijuana, driving under the influence, resisting arrest and leaving the scene of an accident.

"They're reaching on most of these charges but they have a right and the duty to hold him for a preliminary hearing. He'll be okay here at the county lock-up."

The story that emerged, from a brief and tearful meeting between Mitch and his parents, from the police officers, and from Monroe, was that Mitch had an accident involving hitting a pedestrian who had died in the collision.

Mitch claimed that he didn't see or believe that he had hit a person on the dark highway but had had lost control of the truck some hundreds of yards further down the highway and had tested positive for alcohol. He thought it was a bump on the road. He was not drunk but, since he was under 18, he should not have had any alcohol.

In the course of the investigation the cops had searched his truck and found a bag of marijuana. Mitch claimed the weed was not his and that several friends had been in the truck over the last few days and supposed that it belonged to someone else.

Molly and another girl had been in the truck with him and an altercation broke out between the other girl and the arresting officer. Mitch had tried to intervene and that lead to further charges and troubles. The girls had not been charged and their parents had picked them up at the scene.

The truck had a blown a front tire, probably caused by running over a shopping cart. This caused Mitch to lose control and hit a fence. The truck was not seriously damaged, the passengers were okay and the pedestrian was found dying. He was a vagrant but still had a right, of course, to life. Mitch was deemed responsible.

Life changed for the Hunters. Not in a single day, but over time, the accident seemed like a punctuation mark in the life of each family member.

Mom and Dad were terrified for their children and felt that they had come close to losing Mitch to a darker life. What terrible things would have happened to him in jail? They resolved to keep the boys as close as possible for as long as they could. Family time was given more emphasis. Dinner at regular times; everyone expected, guests welcome. Vacations, mainly wilderness-style camping, were scheduled whenever possible.

Mitch paid traffic fines but was not found guilty of the most serious charges. His interest in school declined and he settled for a GED and went to work for his father. Molly graduated and moved to Asheville, North Carolina in order to study ceramics and live with an artsy aunt who welcomed the opportunity to take her in. His feelings of guilt and remorse about the accident were sharp and would never be forgotten.

Mitch declared that he was moving to Asheville on his 18th birthday and Molly was searching for a job on his behalf.

Paul worked with his dad on weekends and, oftentimes, after school. Although he got good grades and was an avid reader, he had no ambition to go to college. His real life was on the job.

Paul began as a laborer. Cleaning up job sites, doing demolition, and, when he got his driving license, running errands. His dad drilled him on the fundamentals of reading blueprints, the math of framing, and the arts of plastering, dry-wall, plumbing and painting. His dad insisted that he got regular haircuts and that he shave every day. "You need to fit in with the other workers Paul. They're conservative, handpicked by me to be respectful of our clients and the properties we work on."

Paul's response was all a father could ask for - compliance with a smile and, "Thanks for the job Dad." Paul loved his father and appreciated all he was learning on the job.

By the time Paul graduated from high school, he was a strong and skilled helper. He earned a good wage and he let his mom salt it away.

With Mitch's hard life lessons, he was not eager to operate a motor vehicle but he eventually got his own pick-up truck and regarded it as a tool for work. He bought the old Chevy from his dad, so he knew that it was in good mechanical condition, albeit a little dinged up. He had scored a few of the dings himself on job sites were conditions were rough. It wasn't as pretty as Mitch's but he kept it very clean.

APRIL 1996

The senior prom was a big dilemma for Paul. He'd had a few crushes and had dated a few girls since his 16th birthday, but did not have a prospect for this valedictorian dance. He consulted with his lunchroom crew and they proposed Sarah Myers.

"Hey. She's hot. No way she'll go with me."

"Really Paul, said Betty. "She doesn't have a boyfriend and you have to talk to her now before someone else snaps her up. Go over there you dope and talk to her."

Paul totally liked the idea of Sarah Myers as a date. He'd had classes with her since starting high school. He thought she was smart and popular. She wore jeans and a tee shirt today for Casual Friday. She was on the slender side with dark eyes and shiny brunette hair. His heart was in his mouth when he approached her in the cafeteria.

Sarah was sitting with 2 other girls and they were surprised when he asked, "Can I sit with you all for a minute?"

"Sure Paul," they murmured while he began a conversation with Sarah.

"Sarah. Say, you know the prom is coming up. I heard that you haven't agreed to go with anyone yet and I was wondering if I could ask you." His pulse was way up but he tried to look calm.

The other girls at the table excused themselves and left. Paul figured that they were sparing his feelings for the turndown.

"Paul. Who said I needed a date?" Sarah gave him an arch look as if she already had more boys wanting to ask her than she knew what to do with.

"Well. I know we haven't seen each other before and I don't have a date. Have mercy. Okay?" He gave her his best smile. "Sarah. Please go with me. I'll get a tux and give you a corsage."

"Well. Why didn't you mention that before?" Her heart was hammering too but she controlled her jitters better than Paul. "Paul, the prom is 4 weeks away. I need you to do me a big favor if I'm going to go with you. I have needs. I need to go on a few dates with you and you have to pick me up at the house and meet my parents. I know it's a lot to ask, but that's my price."

Paul was ecstatic. This was going way better than he'd imagined.

Paul rang Sarah's front doorbell at 5 PM Saturday night. The plan was dinner at the diner and the movies at the triplex – the movie was *Fargo* and they found it darkly appealing. Dinner at the diner was deliberately visible so that their high school cronies would be aware that they'd dated in advance of the prom.

"Paul. Thank you for tonight. I had a lot of fun. The prom is definite then?" She sat rather far away from him, yet in the center of the wide front seat. She looked very appealing in her white scoop-front blouse and tan pedal-pusher pants.

Paul had been trying to avoid looking at her chest all night. Her breasts were totally covered but, in his mind, they were about to leap out at him. "Yes please. I had a good time too and I'm glad we could go out tonight.

"Do you think... I mean, are you free tomorrow afternoon? We could go canoeing at the park. I have all the gear we'd need, paddles, cushions and such. I have my own boat. Mitch, you know, Mitch my older brother, and I bought it a few years ago?"

"What time?"

When their arrangements were complete she leaned slightly toward him and presented him with a glimpse down her blouse pointing to her cheek for a kiss. At the last second she turned her face to his and gave him a full, lip on lip, kiss.

She laughed as she got out of the car, "See Paul. You never know."

He leaped out of the truck to walk her to the door and was rewarded with another cheek. She did not turn toward him this time but he gave her a little pat on the back as she slipped through the door.

"See you tomorrow. Two o'clock. Canoeing." And she was gone.

He remembered the feel of her back as if his hand was still touching her. She felt good, smelled good and was fun. Hell of a combination, he thought as he ran down her drive to jump in his truck. His heart raced and he was out of breath. He had to drive deliberately to calm himself. He was in a hurry to get home, go to bed, and indulge his fantasies.

Canoeing was a big success. Sarah wore a bikini under her shorts and shirt and he was in his bathing trunks. So they were able to cool off in the water after paddling along the banks of Wheeler Lake.

It turned out that Sarah loved jokes. "Knock, knock."

She was in the front of the canoe and he was enjoying a close-up view of her slender back and rounded hips as she plied Mitch's paddle with good energy.

"Who's there?" he sing-songed in response."

"Sam and Janet."

"Sam and Janet who?"

She began singing, to the melody of *Some Enchanted Evening*, "Sam and Janet evening…" she giggled.

"Why do ducks have flat feet?" he asked.

"I dunno. Why?"

"To stomp our forest fires. Why do elephants have flat feet?"

"I don't know. Why?" She looked back at him inquisitively.

"To stamp out flaming ducks!" he roared, laughing.

Sarah splashed him with her paddle and the canoe was a little tippy for a minute, but they managed to keep it together. The jokes were old, but telling them was fun anyway.

At her door he said, "Sarah. I have to work next weekend but I'll be off Sunday afternoon. Want to do something?" He had his hand on her arm and enjoyed the smooth soft skin.

"Sure. How about a picnic by the river, without the canoe, and then home early so's I can get ready for school?"

"Date."

"Date!" She said emphatically, giving him a peck on the lips and a little chest bump. "See you."

Paul was excited to be dating Sarah and he wondered if they would be able to make love. He was certainly eager. But he understood that girls, women, were not so eager. For good reason he thought with the risks of pregnancy and the social stigma of being a loose woman. A slut as they said in school.

But still he hoped, indeed he pined, for the end of his virginal state. He read a book that advocated masturbation before every date - just to take the edge off. Men, the theory went, were more interesting to women if they were less eager. And when the big moment came you'd be less likely to suffer from premature ejaculation. After his first date with Sarah he began a routine involving masturbating as well as shaving, showering, brushing and flossing. It would have embarrassed him to admit this to anyone, but he felt that it helped.

The weather on picnic day was not so hot. It was showery with occasional downpours. They had their sandwiches and drinks under a rustic shelter but the wind was a problem so they ate up and retreated to the cab of the truck. In a few minutes they were hugging and kissing in a state of passion.

She sat in his lap as the windows misted up with condensation inside the cab. He was exploring her breasts, his hand under her strangely flexible bra. He enjoyed her smooth legs with his other hand.

"Sarah. I would really like to make love. I brought these." He dragged out a package of condoms.

"Oh no Paul." She seemed upset. "I just can't!" Her face was flushed and she was breathing funny.

He pulled back in alarm, sure that he had offended her. He began to apologize, "Sarah…"

She interrupted him by pulling him closer, giving him a passionate kiss then whispering in his ear, "Paul. Me too. But I have my period and I just can't make love today. Paul, I really, really like you. We've had so much fun and I like kissing you."

"God damn Sarah. You scared me. I thought I'd gotten out of line and that you were going to blow me off." He relaxed his hold on her and they gazed into each other's face in a loving way.

They continued necking. As they lay across the front seat Sarah said, "Paul. Don't bring those rubbers along when we date. You don't need them. I've been on the pill for a year. My mom insisted, but," she gave him a coy look, "I don't sleep around. It's just a way for my mom to keep me from getting pregnant if I do make love to someone. She likes to plan ahead"

The shadows grew long and they grew weary. And Paul had ejaculated in his pants. Sarah seemed not to notice but, he thought, must have surely suspected when he didn't get out of the car to say goodnight at her house.

Sarah did know of course. She had made sure that he got that little satisfaction. She had felt his body quiver and his muscles writhing as they hugged and she ground her hips against him. She was happy that he was gentle with her.

Paul spent a fair amount on the tux rental and corsage. He was comforted by the sure knowledge that everyone in his class, including Sarah had probably gone through a similar experience. He came down the stairs to the applause of his parents and had to pose for photos. "Paul, you must ask Sarah's parents to share their photos. We want to see you together."

"Okay Mom." He marched proudly from the front door to his truck. He had cleaned it from bumper to bumper for the occasion. His dark brown hair was neatly trimmed and he had shaved even though his beard was still fine.

Sarah's mom answered the door with a smile. "Good evening Paul. Don't you look handsome? Come right in. Sara will be ready in a minute."

"Hi Mr. and Mrs. Myers." Sarah's dad appeared next to his wife and shook Paul's hand with suitable formality.

The 3 sat in the living room until Sarah suddenly appeared in a short, gay, off-the-shoulder formal cocktail dress, and sparkling high heels. Paul was wowed.

"Boy oh boy. Do you look nice! Wow girl."

Sarah paused at the door, smiled and whirled around so that her gown spread out to expose her dancing legs.

Paul shyly presented her with her corsage and her mom pinned it to her dress.

Mom took photos and promised to get double prints for Paul's family.

The couple left the house in Sarah's family SUV. Paul was a little disappointed when the decision was announced but Sarah's dad said that he thought the SUV safer and comfortable for a formal night. Sarah had said, "Please Paul." It had been easy to agree.

They met 3 other couples at the steakhouse and had a gala meal to start the evening. Paul was proud to pay their bill, as he was feeling flush with the pay from several summers' work and the remains of the laundered money he'd stolen with Mitch. It was all safely invested with his mother's supervision.

The Huntsville Marriott was the venue. They used valet parking and posed for a professional photo at the entrance to the ballroom.

The dance was in full swing when they arrived. Paul and Sarah had practiced a little and Paul thought that he was not very good. He surprised himself however and they had a lot of fun. He discovered that she could be comical on the dance floor as well as with jokes. Elbows akimbo, stepping high and wiggling her hips, she was hilarious. She got him to match her moves and they became the center of attention when they performed.

The dance went on until midnight, but they slipped away early.

Paul drove the Myers car respectfully. They went to an upper class neighborhood where his dad was remodeling a lakefront house. He knew the house was vacant and he drove behind it. He backed over a grassy track to the edge of the seawall, next to a beach. Sarah sat close to him and hugged his arm.

The large rolled up quilt and the fact that the seats were down in back to create a carpeted area had not escaped Paul's attention. Sarah had prepared the car and herself with care.

Paul inhaled her perfume as her dress, pantyhose and bra came away. He quickly removed his clothing and they locked in a passionate embrace on top of the soft comforter.

Paul tried to speak to express his feelings but Sarah gently shushed him. Whispering into his ear. "Paul, just do me. Do me now!" She helped him align his engorged penis with her ready vagina.

They made love twice before they had a chance to really appreciate their surroundings. The air was cool, the bright moon shone on the water and there was a beautiful grassy aroma drifting through the night. The leaves rustled softly as the couple lay intertwined, breathing into each other's ears. He was able to see the curves of her thighs, hips and belly. Her dark nipples, standing erect in the moonlight, drew his fingers and his lips. She shuddered with pleasure as he explored her body.

"Paul. You are so beautiful. Thank you for being you."

"I don't know how to say this differently but Sarah I'll always love you and always remember this night and this moment. You are too beautiful for words."

"Me too. Me too you."

Then it got complicated. Sarah was already late for her 1:30 AM curfew. "Paul. I have got to go."

"I know. Just let me hold you one more time." And she did.

A little later they found use for the towels she had thoughtfully rolled into the center of the comforter roll-up.

Redressing was a little awkward. But they looked presentable, perhaps even elegant, when Paul walked her to the front door and she turned her cheek up for a kiss.

He leaned in and she twisted her head quickly to present her lips - but not quick enough. Paul turned his head to press his slightly scratchy cheek into her lips. They laughed loudly just as the porch light turned on and the door opened a crack.

He said "Goodnight Mrs. Myers," to her mom's eye and gave Sarah a peck on the lips before trotting to his truck. It was 2 AM but he felt totally awake and ready for anything. He dropped off to sleep thinking about Sarah's lovely body.

Graduation was held the next Saturday morning in a gala tent on the school grounds. Paul spotted Sarah and waived sadly. Their affair was coming to an end. Sarah was leaving right away to be a summer camp counselor and then would report to The University of Alabama in Tuscaloosa.

They had dinner the night before and Sarah was reserved. She declined the opportunity to "park" with Paul. "Paul. My folks are a little mad at me. Not you. I was late on Saturday and I have to, just have to be home early tonight. I'm sorry," she said with a smile and a tear.

"Paul. Thank you for *promming* me. You saved my life and I love you but I don't think I'll be back home until Thanksgiving and that seems so far away."

"Yeah I guess you're right. Are you saying that you don't want to see me again until you get back?"

"Yes." Sarah's eyes teared up and held his arm. I hate to say it but I think that's best until we figure out a little more about life."

Paul had already confessed to her that he did not want to go to college. He planned to visit Mitch and Molly after graduation and then decide his next moves. He could earn a good living in construction but he wanted to explore other avenues. He was correct when he thought that Sarah was concerned about his lack of direction.

Paul's path was not clear to Sarah. She wanted to be a nurse or other health-care professional. She did not understand Paul's lack of ambition. It scared her that she liked him so well.

PART 2

JUNE 1996

It was beautiful in Asheville. The mountainsides were carpeted with fully greened trees. Flowers bloomed everywhere. It was cool in the mountains unlike Alabama, where summer had already taken charge.

Mitch and Molly rented a one-bedroom apartment near the UNCA campus. They were very proud of their independence. Molly was in an arts program with an emphasis on ceramics. The area was famous for ceramic art and her ambition was to "throw" pots and such for a living. Paul thought that her finished pieces looked good enough to sell anywhere. She beamed when he gave her that opinion.

Paul was crashing on their couch. They made him feel so welcome that he had no hesitation in agreeing to stay for a while. Mitch held his arm for emphasis as he said, "As long as you like little brother."

Molly was busier than Mitch. Her schedule of classes and work was brutal. She worked at the university bookstore. The wage was not high but there were serious benefits. She got discounts on textbooks and merchandise, and, since she was considered to be full time, health insurance and tuition. Her demeanor gave no clue to the frantic pace she kept. She was always smiling and her neat blond hair and placid blue eyes radiated happiness.

Mitch had two jobs involving antiques and collectibles.

He worked at a huge antiques mall named the Cotton Mill. It rented space to dealers who would tag their own merchandise but, in return for a modest rent, they did not have to man their stalls. The mall collected the money from merchandise sales and cut the dealer a weekly check after deducting the rent. Mitch worked for minimum wages plus they let him have several well-located stalls at no cost. He bought inexpensive 'must goes' at negotiated prices and sold them for as much as he could get. He also sold Molly's ceramic work and she was a willing supplier. Her pottery classmates were eager to sell their stuff too, so this was a very good sideline for all concerned.

His second job was to haunt flea markets, yard, and estate sales in his off-time to acquire the 'must goes.' The owner of the Cotton Mill took a shine to him and fed him tips and advice on an ongoing basis. Mitch loved old man Milt Friedman and in an incredibly short time he was making regular profits in addition to his salary.

On this cool Saturday evening, the sun was still hanging over the mountains. The brothers were enjoying a beer while they waited for Molly to get back from Ingles

Supermarket with their dinner. They had comfortable plastic chairs and a little table on their diminutive patio.

"What now little brother? I mean what do you want to do for work now that you're finished with high school? And what about college?"

Paul was not certain. His internal life consisted mostly of trying to forget about Sarah while taking a summer vacation. He enjoyed working for his dad and felt like it was a good learning experience. He had no ambition to study for his own contractor's license.

"I really don't know Mitch. I want to take a few weeks off and then I'll probably go back to Huntsville and work with Dad. I don't feel any money pressure, after all, I'm mooching on you and Molly for a while.

"I've got all my camping gear locked in the truck. Any chance that you and Molly could get away to hang out with me for a bit?"

"I don't think so. I can get away for some day trips but Molly is scheduled at school or work almost every day and needs to rest on her time off. We can ask her though."

Paul gave Mitch a serious look. "Mitch. Do you ever think about the things we did in school? I mean the thefts from Debby's dad and Bohacks. Like the lies we told about the money and all?"

"Sure. I guess we did some crummy things but they were more like adventures than crimes. I'm glad we didn't get caught."

"Yeah. Me too. But I feel guilty about Debby's family disappearing and Bohacks too. I wonder if we were responsible."

"Well. Me too. But we were pretty young. I wouldn't want to do it again. Would you?"

“Hell no! I believe I’m cured.”

“Hi lovers!” Molly called out as she walked up to the patio with paper bags in her short arms. She was a tiny red haired woman with an enormous supply of appealing freckles. They each took a bag and she rewarded them with a hug and a kiss and said, “Dinner in 3 minutes. Then I’m going to crash.”

They ate roast chicken, coleslaw and apple pie still warm from the store’s oven.

“Why don’t you take Paul whitewater canoeing while he’s here Mitch? You love it and he will too. If you go tomorrow I’m only working half a day and I can go check on the stalls at the Mill.” She really wanted to know how her stuff was doing.

“What do you say Paul? We can go to Clancy, Georgia and rent a whitewater canoe. Do you have our paddles?”

“Yep. I mean yes to the paddles. Canoeing sounds great but I’ve never done white water. Is it like that old movie *Deliverance* with Burt Reynolds?”

“It’s way more fun and there are no mean hillbillies,” Mitch laughed. “We won’t need a reservation since it’s a weekday. You’re gonna love it.”

Molly and Mitch were right. Paul loved the whitewater experience. Mitch rented a two-man canoe with big airbags in the bow and stern for floatation and special saddles to keep their weight low in the boat. There were foot braces and thigh straps to keep them in the boat when it bucked in the rapids. The straps were adjusted for easy exiting in case they spilled.

It was a two-and-one-half hour drive from Asheville to the little town of Clancy. There were continuous mountain vistas as they rolled along through deep country with few towns and villages. The roads were great and traffic was sparse. Paul felt at peace in the mountain terrain. He told Mitch that he was missing his girlfriend and how they had parted. Sarah's somewhat hasty departure from his life became a little less painful as he shared the story with his brother.

Mitch listened until Paul was talked out. "Bro. You'll get over it. Today, on the river, there won't be any room in your head for negativity. Only joy and terror."

That seemed a little strong to Paul but he knew that Mitch was joking about the fear - he hoped. He already felt good about the day.

There were 2 options for paddling the Clancy River from the town of Clancy: upstream or downstream. They chose up because they wanted to end up near their truck that was parked at the outfitter's take-out beach.

The outfitter that rented them the canoe provided transportation upstream to a public put-in area on the Clancy River.

They carried the boat to a practice pond near the drop-off place. They got in the boat and Mitch drilled Paul on what he'd have to do on the river. Paul learned to paddle on the left side of the boat with his right hand firmly on top of the paddle. He practiced paddling on both sides of the boat without shifting his hand position so that he could shift sides as fast as possible with a minimum of commotion. He learned the high and low braces and sweeps to help turn the boat in either direction. He had good natural balance, no fear of the water and the strength and flexibility of his hardworking, youthful body.

"Mitch. How did you learn to paddle like this?"

"In Asheville. The first job, that Molly got me, was a seasonal gig with a canoe rental outfit on the French Broad River. I was mostly a cashier and 'Yard Monkey' because they were a little leery of my driving record. The folks there took me in hand on my days off and taught me the basics.

"I could be a guide and trip leader there but it's seasonal and I needed a steady job. I'm saving to open my own business when Molly graduates from college. I think it'll be next year. Mr. Friedman, my boss will give me a steer when I'm ready."

"Wow Mitch. You're going to get rich. Molly too. Are you two planning to get married?"

"Yes and no. Yes but we don't want to set a date until she gets out of school and learns what her options are. I really love her, but we're getting along great just now and I don't want to push her. She's the boss you know."

They were soon on the river. There the light, fresh smell of the water, the lush forest odors and shifting shadows transformed Paul into a whitewater devotee in minutes. He liked the feel of the boat as they powered along with their old wood paddles. He was aware of the cold splash of the water, the moving wind and brilliant sunshine when they were out of the shadow of overhanging trees.

An idea formed in Paul's mind. He began to see a path for the next few months. He would find a way to camp near the river, buy a boat and get a job. He would be on his own for the first time in his life.

He knew that it was a juvenile plan but he shrugged his mental shoulders and said, what the hell Paul. I'm young and life is long.

Mitch agreed that it wasn't much of a plan and somewhat lacking in goals. "But Paul, it's okay. Where do you think you can camp for free?"

"That's the 64 cent question wise one. I don't know. I'm not broke. Just ugly. If I only score 2 out of 3 of my wishes, I'll be happy for a while."

Paul got a resounding 3 for 3 on his wish list.

He returned to Clancy a few days later and began shopping for a boat. He asked about work at every enterprise on both banks of the river as he moved upstream from the village of Clancy.

No one needed help but he found a boat for sale. A handsome Mohawk canoe, rigged for white water and not bruised up. It sat on sawhorses, bottom-up, next door to a little eatery called The Barbecue Shack with a 'For Sale' placard taped to its red side.

The Shack could be seen and approached from the river as well as the road. There were no immediate neighbors on the road or on the other side of the river. Just trees. People ordered food through a window with a generous stainless steel shelf and could use the benches and picnic tables scattered about.

He rapped on the closed service window and heard someone approach from inside.

A cheerful woman in a spotted apron and chef's white jacket stepped through the door. She looked a little stocky in her cooking outfit and her red hair was trying to escape the confines of its hairnet. Up close she smelled like cooking smoke. She smiled and said, “We open at 11:30.”

“Ma’am. I just want to ask you about the boat. How much is it?”

“Oh. Good,” now she was really grinning. She came out and they walked to the boat together.

“I just put it out here today. I decided that I’m never going back out on that danged river again.” She hitched up her shorts a little to show him a very big bruise that went up her leg, out of sight. “I thought I’d get beat to death before I could drown properly. Never again!” She laughed. “Help me roll it over so you can see inside.

“I paid 600 bucks for it when I bought this place a year ago. I thought I’d found paradise.

“It’s fully rigged as you can see. Air bags, bow and stern. Saddle and leg straps. It’s had very little wear.”

The boat looked indestructible. Large floatation air bags were laced into the bow and stern. The center cockpit was dominated by a kind of saddle for the paddler to sit on. It allowed the operator to sit lower than the built-in thwart seats that were made of a pretty varnished wood.

“Yeah. This is a very nice boat. I’ve seen the Mohawk brand before.” He walked around the boat petting it as he went.

“Say. My name’s Paul Hunter. I’d like to make an offer.”

“Megan Smith. But I won’t take a cent less.”

“Megan. I’m looking for a place to camp and this is real nice by the river here. I don’t know how long I want to stay but could I give you your asking price and you throw in permission to park over there at the edge of your parking lot and pitch my tent by the river, out of sight, for a while."

"I don't know, er…Paul."

"I could give you a $100.00 cash deposit and a check for the balance."

Megan was not convinced. Paul looked like a nice guy but she didn't know if it was even legal to camp there.

"I don't know. Where would you go to the bathroom?"

Paul thought he'd just use the abundant woods but Megan had a point.

"Megan. Let me sweeten the offer. I'll use your facility," he pointed to the single door that was marked 'His'n n' Her's.' If you'll let me use the bathroom, I'll take responsibility for cleaning it up every day. Keep it clean. I'm sure that's a chore you'd rather not do."

Megan was 34 years old and escaping from a bad marriage. Her planning and execution of the change from city office worker to rural free spirit was not without complications.

The barbecue business was working financially, but the work and the hours were long and hard. Paul struck a note when he offered more than just money for her little boat. She sensed the possibility of an even better outcome. Megan was ready to accept the deal – Paul pitching his tent and using her bathroom, but she was moved to say, "Paul. I like your offer but there's one more thing you could do that would make it work for me."

"Uh oh. What is it?"

"First I need to ask you some questions. I need to know who you are and where you are from and what you have been doing."

Paul explained that he had just graduated from high school and that he had worked for his dad in construction. She asked him to write his parents' and Mitch's names, addresses and telephone numbers on a lined pad. She asked him for references and all he could think of were his bank, his high school Lit teacher and the pastor of the church they attended on holidays. He wrote the contact information on the yellow pad.

She seemed satisfied.

"Paul. This business is a little too much for me. Do you think you could work one day a week for me? Minimum wage plus tip jar. And I want you to pick up the parking lot trash every day? For that you can camp here, use the restroom and, on your one day of hourly work, you can eat your lunch and dinner on the house."

Paul grinned and offered his hand. "Great Megan. I promise to do all that. When do you want me to start?"

"Today. You can pitch your tent. Give me a check for the boat now, and I'll let you know what day I want you to work. I need to think it over. I'm assuming you don't care too much. I mean about which day."

Paul went to a payphone at the Caverns Outdoor Center. The center was a big whitewater raft rental, restaurant, and motel complex a few miles downriver. He soon learned to call it COC. He called his parents and Mitch to let them know where he was and what he was doing.

"Mom. I'll be home when it gets cold here. Give Dad my love. And," he laughed, "yes I'll send you 10% of my paycheck. Don't expect much."

COC was the largest enterprise around. He had lunch in a restaurant there; one of the 3 restaurants on the property. The café was named 'The Take Out' because it was close to a sandy beach where rafters pulled their boats out of the water after running the last big rapid of the run. There were plenty of customers, mostly family groups just off the river and hungry for something warm. Paul liked its homey feel.

He snooped around and found that the public restroom there had showers and he supposed that he could use them if he liked. There were no posted signs to the contrary.

There was a mailbox on the wall near the office for the little hotel attached to the center. He asked the woman at the motel desk in the office if they sold stationary. He was given a piece of copy paper and an envelope. She sold him a stamp. He wrote:

Hi Sarah

I think about you every day. Wish you were here.

Hope you are having a beautiful summer at Camp Karamac.

I just bought a canoe and found a part-time job at a barbecue joint that will let me spend time learning to be a whitewater paddler. I'll be camping by the Clancy River - it's really nice here. See you in the fall.

XXX OOO Paul

Paul erected his tent on a flat spot well above the river. It was not visible from the road or from the barbecue shack parking lot. One would have to get very close to catch a glimpse of it.

He rigged a line over the limb of a tree to haul food supplies off the ground. He didn't want to attract a bear or the skunks and raccoons that were famous for their thievery. He did not want a fire pit. His one-burner propane camp stove and a propane lantern were enough. He'd be content with the simplest of diets but hot coffee was a blessing in the morning.

It rained that first night and he woke wet in the morning. He had failed to dig a trench on the up-slope, above his tent, to divert ground water. The price of this oversight was wet bedding that had to be spread out to dry. He was philosophical about it. He reckoned that he'd make a few more mistakes before he learned to live without a house. He moved the tent to let it dry in the sunshine.

After he used and cleaned the restroom, he patrolled the parking area for litter, and tamped down the trash already in the large containers. Megan watched him approvingly through the service window with the built-in stainless steel counter.

"Hi Paul. Thank you for a job well begun. Paul. Would you mind working on Wednesdays? I want to go to Asheville and spend time with some friends. If you will spend tomorrow with me, I'll show you everything you need to know. I'll spend the night in town and be back on Thursday morning. That'll be our regular schedule. Okay?

"Oh. And I'll pay you for the training time. But Wednesday will be your regular day from morning light until dark. I'm just going to pay you cash. Is that okay?"

Paul nodded an enthusiastic yes. "That'll be great. Say Megan, today's Monday. Right?"

Paul was an apt student. They began in the screened room she called the chophouse. Megan started each day by loading pork butts in a stainless steel smoker above a wood fire lit with a built-in gas ignition system. She then made coleslaw and heated large cans of beans on a 2-burner stove.

"Follow this list Paul." She handed him a handwritten list of daily chores arranged in the correct sequence. "I've learned how much prep to do each day and it usually works out. If I run out I just apologize and folks are generally okay with that. I mean I just can't stop and make coleslaw or smoke a new batch of pork butts when I'm by myself with a line at the window.

"The menu is simple: pulled pork sandwiches; pulled pork platter with baked beans; bread and slaw; hot dogs and hamburgers. They can order anything to drink as long as it begins with a 'lemon' and ends with an '*ade*.'" They laughed at her little joke.

She showed him how to handle the lemonade powder, how to apply the dry spice rub to the pork before slow cooking in the smoker. She taught him to preposition trays of little paper cups of barbecue sauce. Her barbecue sauce, baked beans enhancement, and coleslaw recipes were taped to the refrigerator door for him. Other condiments were in plastic pouches including sauerkraut and diced onions.

She showed him how to clean and sanitize the chophouse, the hot dog steamer, the hot table and all the associated gear. Thin burgers were cooked to order on a small grill.

"I usually clean the chophouse before opening but, if I get busy with something else, it may have to wait until closing."

The last thing she did each day was to haul all the garbage to the county garbage station a few miles up the road. She had a heavy workload and Paul admired the cheerful face she put on everything – especially with customers. He decided to haul the trash for her even on his days off.

Paul's Wednesday was relatively easy. He bagged the cash register tapes and cash before locking up and hauling the trash. The vinyl bank envelope was hidden behind the big #10 cans of beans. He guessed that Megan did her banking on Wednesdays.

There was still some daylight left when his work was finished. He dragged his canoe into the water. He braced himself and turned the boat downstream in the lee of a rock so that he could accelerate into the faster moving water. This was his 4th outing in the boat and he was getting good at self-rescue because he flipped the boat at some point during every trip. It was a hard learning process.

Two air bags filled the entire bow and stern spaces of the sturdy boat. Nylon laces served kept them in place to prevent water from filling the canoe when it flipped. There were stainless steel eyes screwed into the gunwale and thwarts to help tie down loose gear such as watertight bags filled with lunches, cameras, wallets, keys, and such.

He leaned the wrong way. Again! And found himself immersed in the cold water, gathering up his bow rope and paddle in his left hand and stroking for shore with his right hand. The water was not moving fast, but he had to watch for rocks as he floated with the current, and use his feet to push off those that came close. He knew not to try and stand up in waist-deep water but it was soon shallow enough to let him plant his feet on the bottom and haul his water filled canoe to shore. He was bruised from bumping into underwater boulders. The water was freezing. He thought he'd buy a wet suit when Megan paid him.

He was not upset. He knew that, counter to his intuition, he had to lean and paddle on the downstream side when leaving calm water on the shore and turning into the current. I can do this he muttered while rolling his boat upside down to empty the water. He was back in business in a few minutes and managed the rest of the short run with pleasure.

He expected to learn a lot by the end of the season. He wanted to hook up with paddlers who would suggest other, more challenging rivers. He would be glad to provide transportation as an inducement for others to make the journeys with him. But the Clancy was his favorite, his only, river for now. He eddied out behind rocks, surfed standing waves and rode the bigger rapids down to COC. There he left his boat on the shore, bought a soda and hitched a ride back upstream to return in his truck to retrieve the canoe.

He was in bed soon after sundown. He closed his eyes to dream of Sarah. He drifted off remembering her feel, her smell, and the sound of her voice as she said "Do me now…"

Some days Paul would go upstream to the most distant put-in and Paddle all the way to Clancy. After a few weeks he became familiar with some of the regular paddlers. They were mostly kayakers who thought of canoes as less than hip. Nevertheless, he did make friends, and was delighted to learn better boat handling techniques and river lore. He decided that he'd sell his canoe at the end of the season at COC's Guest Appreciation Festival at the end of October and start the next spring off with a kayak. There was no shortage of advice on this subject.

His new friend Marvin Redman told him, "COC sells most of their boats at the festival. They start fresh in the spring with new rafts. The rafts are used heavily and soon display patches and scars. They're tough boats, those used ones, and will last an individual owner for many years. But the patches are not good for the company's image."

Marvin worked for COC in the kitchen of The Take Out Café. He was very short, almost a midget, it seemed to Paul. But he was dark and powerfully built and very manly with a full beard and copious body and arm hair visible. His beautiful, natural kindness drew him to accept Paul, the outsider, as a friend, and Paul liked and appreciated him very much.

The 2 men sat in their boats in the quiet water behind a large flat rock. The sky and river filled Paul's senses. They were face to face for easy conversation while they waited for the rest of their party to catch them. Each man had a hand on the others gunwale and the boats bumped together with a little hollow sound. Marvin's kayak was scarred up from hard use. Paul's red canoe was clean and new looking.

Marvin was explaining, "…but for rafting companies to put 2 seasons' use on a boat is not their best course. The employees buy their boats through the COC retail operation and get enough of a break on the price that they can sell them at the end of the year and just about break even. The reason I don't do the sale thing every year is that I think it's better for the planet to use our possessions until they're worn out."

Paul laughed. "I was wondering why so many paddlers had raggedy shorts and sandals held together with tape."

"Yep. That's it. Sort of a cult. I think that's the COC ideal – like taking a vow of poverty when a priest joins joins the church."

Through Marvin and his friends, who were now Paul's paddling buddies, Paul learned that Caverns Outdoor Center was a good place to work. The company mission statement declared that it was a community of athletes and philosophers. Good caretakers of the environment and a sort of disdain for money. Marvin laughed, "That means that the pay is lousy – don't ask for a raise."

COC was a seasonal operation from April through October. The mountain air was too cold for safe paddling in the off-season although, being in the South, there were many nice days in the winter. Snow fell often as moist air masses moved north from the Gulf of Mexico. But it didn't usually linger too long. Starting on the first of November the area would be quiet and almost deserted. Along the river only The Take Out Restaurant operated on a limited schedule. The Barbecue Shack would close too. Marvin would work at The Take Out Restaurant on a limited schedule.

"Paul. If you want to work for COC put your application in before the end of the season. You can use Megan and me as references. You'll be glad you did it.

You know the work will be hard but you'll have a lot more paddling friends and you can bunk in staff housing. That will be more comfortable than that raggedy-ass tent of yours."

"Thanks Marvin. I have a slightly different vision. I spoke with Megan and she'll let me camp at her place whenever I want. I'm going to take the raft guide course at COC in March. I'll use the lodging offered by the school during the course week and sign up as a reserve raft guide on the Clancy River. She'll work with me on scheduling so's I can work for her 1 or 2 days a week then work whenever I can get guide work at the center. I don't need a more regular job because my expenses are close to zero and winter construction work with my dad pays well.

"Maybe I can get a regular job at COC the year after. I gotta keep moving up because I'm near the bottom now. And I'm loving it."

Marvin thought it was a good plan. As a senior COC employee he didn't earn much but with staff housing, a working wife, and low expenses he felt rich. "I love cooking and I love paddling. My wife and I aren't getting along so well though. She wants me to get a real job. Go figure. More money but no time to enjoy it."

The summer slipped away and autumn colors and the smell of chimney smoke tickled the senses. Paul had not shaved since the prom. His beard was dark but he kept it trimmed with scissors that had become a part of his kit. He was used to living rough and his was getting stronger and building muscle mass from paddling and work. He had plenty of free time so he was able to take frequent hikes on the nearby Appalachian Trail.

Paul was very happy to see October coming to an end. It was getting too cold to live in the tent and his last day with Megan was scheduled for October 30th. He planned to sell the canoe at the COC Guest Appreciation Festival. Molly and Mitch invited him to visit in Asheville and his dad was more than ready for him to get back to a real job. Life, Paul thought, was good.

He was canoeing alone one brilliant autumn day. The hardwood trees were dressed in gay hues of red and yellow. He made frequent turns into minor eddies trying to be totally technical with his strokes and balance. He was practicing whitewater skills. Just behind a half-boat sized rock, he nosed into the bank only to find a screen of bushes that masked a side stream entering the Clancy. He pushed his way in with a couple of light strokes.

It was a flat area and the shallow water was crystal clear. It was just inches deep. His boat floated above river stones and pebbles strewn on the bottom. Grasses and bushes screened the wilderness garden from sight in every direction.

He stepped out of the boat to look around and wound up sitting on the mossy bank, basking in the sun. There was a carpet of green moss in the dappled sunlight and the rustle of leaves.

He liked the peaceful spot so well that he always, thereafter, paddled there when he was by himself. It was his chilling spot, his private paradise. Sometimes he fell asleep. Sometimes he just daydreamed about his life and where he was going.

NOVEMBER 1996

Thanksgiving was a bust. Sarah disappointed him. They spoke on the phone the Friday morning after Thanksgiving. She seemed older and remote and her words shocked Paul, "Paul. It's over with us. I want to be in school without any entanglements and you are a definite entanglement.

"You know that I love you and what we had in High school, but I can't see any future for us. I'm going to be a nurse and marry a doctor. I know that sounds shallow but I want you to have it straight. That is my dream."

Paul had suspected that it was over with Sarah but he held out hope until the end of the call. She declined his invitation to meet for lunch. He felt that high school was a very long time ago.

Paul was so sad that evening that he broke down and told his mother, "Mom, I thought about her all summer and wanted to go back to the way we were but she wouldn't even talk about it. She's husband-shopping at the medical school." His eyes welled up and he was glad to bury his head in his mother's shoulder.

She gave him every comfort a mother could. "Paul. You'll soon be over this. There are many women in our wonderful world and you will find the one meant for you. You'll know when you're ready"

"Thanks Mom. I think you're right. I'm not ready for a relationship. I was wrong. Sarah and I were not thinking in the same track at all. I'll wise up after a while."

Paul went to work for his father with the understanding that he would have the boating season off to take his River Guide Course and spend the summer in Clancy. He telephoned Megan to confirm their previous deal and she seemed fine with the prospect having her Wednesdays off again next season.

The winter sped by. Paul fell in love with a slightly used kayak he bought at the local outfitter store. On warmer weekend days, he donned wetsuit and neoprene boots to practice in Huntsville's rivers for summer on the Clancy River.

SPRING 1997

The 3rd week of March was relatively balmy in the mountains of North Georgia. There was lots of sun and only a few snow flurries. His weeklong training class as a river guide exceeded his expectations. There was a mix of instruction including short, indoor classroom theory and long days outside, in all weather, learning everything one could know about running whitewater rivers in rafts. He learned how to maintain them on the river. Guest satisfaction and safety were a big part of the program.

There were 18 male students and 6 females. Some were trained professionals including an ER physician, a CPA, a police lieutenant and a high school teacher with a MBA. This lot all professed to want more adventure and less money. They were willing to live in poverty (staff housing) as a part of a package that enabled them to spend days on the rivers in good company.

Lucy Lu, the ER doctor, a young Chinese woman, told Paul, “I can work full time here and odd shifts in my hospital in Atlanta. Maybe just one 24-hour shift a week, will keep my position. Off-season I can work normal shifts at the hospital.”

The CPA planned to work his profession only during tax season. Each of the professionals was making a financial sacrifice. Each had a different story.

COC provided all the gear the students needed including wet suits, first aid kits and rescue bags. The bags included a variety of ropes to help haul people and boats out of the water. The students learned to manage heavy rafts full of inept guests with paddles but without skills, perform rescues and avoid dangerous situations before they developed. He was told that most whitewater injuries were inflicted by novice boaters hitting one another with paddles. The course was much more intense than his high school studies.

Paul spent a happy week with Mitch and Molly in Asheville. Mitch was more prosperous and talking about a shop of his own.

He returned to working for Megan one day a week. His first day was a Wednesday on the 2nd of April. The river gorge area was not busy in the spring but she liked having a day off. Since the days were short and the nights cold, he spent as little time in his tent as possible. Oftentimes he spent hours drinking coffee at The Take Out Restaurant or doing errands in town. The laundry was one of his favorite places because of the warmth of the driers and occasional company from COC employees on a similar mission. He saw every movie within a 50-mile radius.

Paul took a 2-day class at the YMCA's swimming pool in Atlanta to learn the Eskimo roll. This one maneuver made kayaking much easier and safer than canoeing. The roll enabled him to stay in the boat and turn himself upright whenever he capsized.

When he made a mistake he could recover without having to deal with a boat full of water or total immersion. His life vest and helmet offered him a good deal of protection from rocks. The deadliest whitewater threat was foot entrapment in rocks and crevices hidden by moving water. In a kayak, his Eskimo-roll techniques meant that his feet were likely to spend less time on the river bottom. Marvin began giving Paul kayak tips on their days off.

Paul hung out at the COC rafting area on weekends hoping to get work as a guide. He made sure that they knew he was there and that they had him on the list of accredited guides. He got his inauguration trip in the first week of May. COC paid him a flat $20.00 and he collected $40.00 in tips from 6 happy passengers. Regular guides would get 3 or even 4 trips on lucky days.

As they pushed off he told his guests that it was his first trip down the river as a paid guide. His passengers felt a frisson of unease when they heard those words.

His confident manner of instructing them and guiding the boat down the first few rapids allayed their worries and they were soon engulfed in the whitewater experience. He was a hit and he loved the job. He would get a trip every few days but it required time and effort. He looked just like all the other guides with well-worn river shoes and khaki shorts. He bought a Tilly floating hat and sunglasses. His guests always wanted to have their pictures taken with him after the raft trips - especially the girls and children.

SUNDAY, MAY 18, 1997

A huge rain event occurred in mid-May. Megan arrived at his tent at nine in the morning to find him re-digging the moat that led water away from the tent. His breath was visible in the cold morning air. He was muddy and a little out of sorts. The tent was fighting the wind.

Megan pulled up in her little truck and jumped out shouting. "Paul! Come quick. The ceiling of my trailer is collapsing and I can't get the tarp in place by myself! I've got leaks and there's a branch lying on top." Megan was breathing hard and on the verge of tears. She wore a yellow raincoat and matching hat. She was mud splattered.

His mood changed in an instant. "Let's take my truck," he said. "I've got tools and stuff in the back." They made their way to her simple home place a mile upriver from the Barbecue Shack.

Her site was a beautiful cut into a mountainside. It was on a side road a few hundred feet away from the main route. Its principal feature was a long view of the Clancy River. The river was brown with silt this day and the muddy approach to her driveway was not easy.

The house was a 32-foot, 1-bedroom, house trailer. He had been there before to help her with chores. He and Marvin had built a deck and steps for her on their day off last fall. The deck was 12 feet on each side and not far off the ground so there was no rail. It comfortably held a table, four redwood dining chairs and a park bench.

The first problem was that there was a rather large tree limb on the roof. It was still attached to a tree that leaned over the dwelling. "It scared the hell out of me when it hit just before dawn. Bam! I fell out of bed."

A large blue tarp was partly unfolded and just sitting in the water and mud at the bottom of her steps. There was a clothes line tied to the grommet in one corner.

"I just couldn't handle it," she croaked. "Do you think we can do it together?"

He peeked around to the back of the trailer and confirmed his suspicion that the ground was too slick and steep to just climb up to cut the branch away.

"Sure," Paul reassured her, "But it'll take a little doing. I've either got to get on the roof or climb the bank with my saw. I want to try the bank first and I'll need your help."

He dove into the space behind his front seat. He emerged with a braided polypropylene rope he kept for river emergencies. It was rigged inside a weighted throw bag. He took his carpenter's saw from the back and led the way.

"Come on Megan. Follow me." He scrambled to get to the narrow space between the bank and the trailer, reaching his hand back to help her along. He paused directly below the offending tree's trunk. The base of the tree was out of reach 10 feet above their heads.

She held the saw while he gently tossed the weighted rope to get it around the base of the tree and fall back to his feet. The rope enabled him to scramble to the base of the tree. He reached back for the saw. He couldn't reach the crotch where the branch had snapped so he put the saw down, pulled the rope until he had enough to work with. He tied the saw, through the handle with a hitch that let him carry it on his back while he climbed the tree and cut the offending limb free.

The cold rain continued to fall while she anxiously watched his progress. They were soaked despite their rain gear and hats.

"It won't be pretty Megan," he said, "but we'll get it done." He cut the offending limb close to the trunk.

He dropped the saw to the ground and again used his rescue rope to snag the now-severed tree limb.

"Let's carry this rope to the end of the trailer and start pulling. See if we can get the branch off."

As hard as they pulled and worked the rope the branch didn't move. Paul wound up tossing it over the trailer and wrapping the end around his trailer hitch. They used the truck's horsepower to get the branch to the ground.

"Okay," he grinned at her. "Let's cover the roof." Their faces were streaming with rain.

The tarp took a good deal of effort and time. There was a blustery wind accompanying the rain. And it caused the large tarp to balloon and flap furiously, the corners flying threateningly about their heads. By noon they had managed to spread it over the trailer's roof and had it tied down with clothesline through the grommets.

Although Megan hadn't been up to doing the morning's jobs by herself, she had proven herself agile and fit. Now, at the end of the rescue projects, she was emerging as the leader again.

They were wet, chilled and dirty. To Paul, she seemed younger, small, and in need of care.

"Paul. You can't go back to your tent in this mess. Come in and clean up while I fix us something to eat. I'll make coffee too."

Things looked normal inside the trailer. Megan pointed to a puddle on the kitchen floor. "The water must have come in near the ceiling," she said. "I think the crack is behind the ceiling paneling and cabinets."

Paul noticed a slight distortion in the ceiling and said, "I'll have a look under the ceiling panel after I get cleaned up. Might be something really simple."

His clothes were in an impossible state of grime. "Here Paul," she grinned impishly. "Take my bathrobe and hand me out your muddy stuff. I'll put it in the washer." She bustled around while he stepped into her shower and bathed.

The only problem was that after his wash, her robe was too small and a tad too pink. What the heck, he thought, at least I'm dry and warm. Megan had waited for him to emerge from the bathroom before starting the washer. She had changed her clothing and combed her hair.

"Have some coffee and a roll," she said as she stepped into the bathroom. She was smiling over at his somewhat comical predicament of being stuck without his clothing. "You'll have to hang out here with me for a while. And by the way, there's no way I can even try to do business today."

After couple of cups of hot coffee and a pair of big sandwiches they sat on the couch with their feet up.

"Paul. Would you watch a movie with me? I've got *Quest For Fire* in the machine. Okay." She did not get any reception from broadcast stations and cable had not reached her branch yet.

The rain continued and Paul noticed that the puddle on the floor was not smaller. "Let me take a look at the ceiling first. See if there's anything I can do." He dragged a chair to the middle of the floor and stepped up, too late realizing that he would suffer a complete loss of modesty when he reached over his head and the robe rode up. He paused, embarrassed. Megan stood next to the chair, interested in what he'd find.

Megan saw his problem. "Here Paul, let me help you with that." She pulled the robe's hem down as he reached up. Trouble was she did this one handed and placed her other hand on the back of his thigh and slid it higher as he began to raise his arms.

Paul felt a little unbalanced at this development and placed a hand on her head for balance. He looked down and saw only beauty. There was a pause in home repairs. They moved to the sofa for the unveiling of their bodies and to the bedroom for the ravishment. Her shorts and tee landed on top of the robe on the floor.

Paul was amazed and Megan was delighted.

In her case she had been without a man for two years and had been happy enough with that. Her life was challenging and this development with Paul had not been her intention. It was an impish impulse that took her by surprise. She was 33-years old and in the best condition of her life. Megan was ready for love before the robe hit the floor.

Paul was too surprised for words. He had thought of Megan an adult woman, well above his status as an 18-year-old recent high school grad. But he had become aroused the minute her hand had moved to his thigh and doubly inspired as he looked down at his hand on her head. Her clear face, shiny hair and eloquent eyes galvanized his nerve endings. She was a desirable woman and he acted like a man.

Sated after their third round of intercourse, they lay naked in her bed as the wind buffeted the walls and the rain pinged on the roof. He toyed with her nipples and she burrowed her face into his neck.

"Paul," she declared, "That was something. You are a bull my young friend."

"Thanks Megan. You too…" She giggled.

"No. Not that. I mean you are a wonderful lover. You know I've never made love in a bed before. S'funny, I didn't know how nice it could be. I don't want to leave."

"I don't want you to go either, but there is a problem."

"What's that?"

"You know. I'm old enough to be your mother. Today was priceless. I wouldn't change a thing, but I'm at least 15 years older than you are and this is just a fling for you. A thing that is good. But not a thing that will last beyond a day, or a week, or maybe this summer. We can have lots of fun but our life needs are different. You need a girl to fall in love with you and have babies."

"Yeah. But I'm confused about something."

"What?"

"Can't you have babies?" he said with a leer."

She leaned back slapped his shoulder - hard. "Damn right buddy. But not with you – you're a baby yourself."

"Am not!" he shouted and rolled her over and began to spank her buttocks. She scrambled to get away. He got in a few good licks and her cheeks turned pink before she could sit on them to make him stop.

They laughed at the horseplay but a note of sadness gripped them too. Paul knew that she was right. "Well Megan, that may be true," he said ruefully. "But I'd give anything to spend the night with you. They hugged. They slept. They ate more sandwiches. They made love again and then they watched *Quest For Fire*.

It was a rowdy movie about cavemen and survival. Rae Dawn Chong was costumed only in blue dye. She played the role of a homo-sapiens girl interacting with a bunch of Cro-Magnon people. They loved the movie.

Paul decided that he was having the best night of his life. He was reluctant to sleep. Lying with soft, sweet smelling Megan was so much better than his usual hard, rock lined, sleeping arrangements, that he could not wipe the smile off his face.

MONDAY, MAY 19, 1997

They woke late, gazing at each other in the morning glow filtering through her bedroom's skylight. The day was clear and the sun was just coming over the mountain. She declined his advances, whispering, "Wait Paul. I'm a little sore down there."

He nodded understanding.

"Let me make you feel good." Her face descended and her hands and lips began stroking his chest and then his belly. She engulfed his morning erection with tender lips and gentle hands. "Paul," she murmured, "just lie on your back and let me do the work."

Her hair was soft on his skin and he floated in ecstasy until, at length, he exploded in her mouth grasping her hair with both hands to prolong and deepen the penetration. "Oh my God Megan. Oh my God…"

She released him when he began to squirm, and wiped her face along his body as she sought his lips and strong embrace. “That was a gift my friend she breathed. Thank you for being you.”

Paul just kissed and hugged her in a loving way. The taste and stickiness of his ejaculation made the kissing and embrace even more intimate. This was officially the best morning of his life.

Megan’s washer and drier did their magic. Paul showered and dressed in his clean jeans and tee shirt. She now wore the pink robe.

He got back up on the kitchen chair and loosened a ceiling panel to reveal a sharp branch tip poking through the insulation and outer skin of the trailer. He pushed it out, observing that the hole was minor. He pounded the jagged edge of the break with the rubber handle of his hammer and replaced the insulation and tile. They had not noticed the puncture when they were putting the tarp in place.

“I’ll have to get up there with some repair goop.

“Say Megan. Was there a repair kit when you got this thing?”

She gave him the key to the exterior storage spaces and he found a can of black glue and a metal panel intended to fix the kind of damage the unit had suffered. He remembered a 2x8 plank stashed behind the trailer, where they had walked the day before. He leaned it against the roof and used it as a monkey-walk ramp. On the roof, under the tarp, he saw a small depression where the tree had punctured the roof. He was able to pop the ding out with a little ingenuity and a piece of wire. He applied the patch neatly despite the stickiness of the black goop he was using to plug the hole and bond things together.

The tarp was dry now from sitting in the sun. Together they folded it and stowed in an outside, built-in storage compartment.

They had coffee and cereal and a kiss goodbye. "Paul. Take me to my truck. You'll be working Wednesday and then I'll see you on Thursday."

TUESDAY, MAY 20, 1997

He whiled away the day working on his tent and trying to get his feet back on the ground. Holy Moly! he mused. Why had he not noticed before that Megan was so hot? And how can we get together like that again?

Paul's tent and gear were a wet mess. He spent the day taking care of his stuff, cleaning the restaurant bathroom and policing its parking lot. He was able to smile and wave to Megan who appeared in the service window from time to time. They would have to talk, he mused. Where could this go for them?

Megan closed shop and walked over to Paul where he sat on a log outside his tent. "Paul honey. I'll be in Asheville tomorrow and I need the night off. I'm bushed."

"Me too," he grinned at her as she sat next to him.

"I'll be home late and we need to talk. So. How about dinner at my place Thursday night? You provide it.

Okay. Just a pizza would be fine. Anything but barbecue or coleslaw."

She gave him a peck and a pat and they parted. He went to have supper at The Take Out Restaurant and, afterwards, went right to bed. He had sweet dreams about making love to Megan. In his dream it was raining hard and they were trying to make a baby.

WEDNESDAY, MAY 21, 1997

The day was normal. Not too busy and plenty of time to think. He planned the Thursday dinner. Definitely not pizza. Maybe a couple of candles and a bunch of flowers to tell Megan how much he cared for her.

Paul planned to go paddling Thursday morning – all the way to town. He envisioned a nice solo to Clancy to do grocery shopping. He wanted to buy some shaving cream and aftershave lotion, thinking he'd be sexier without facial hair.

Despite being alone much of the time, he was in contact with his paddling buddies most days and interacted with customers every Wednesday. He had learned to treasure solitude when he could manage it.

THURSDAY, MAY 22, 1997

Paul's run down the river to Clancy was totally enjoyable. He pushed off early and stopped to surf on standing waves and major eddies along his way.

He got a haircut and the barber threw in a professional shave for an additional five bucks. This was a first for Paul. Later, his face was glowing, as he cruised the supermarket aisles.

He toted his grocery bags to the kayak and left them in the cockpit while he hitched a ride to his vehicle. He was always gratified by how easy it was to travel by thumb in this area.

He was surprised when Megan's truck was not in place when he arrived at his tent. She must have been delayed in Asheville, he thought as he drove the few miles to The Take Out Restaurant for a late lunch. It was not busy and he enjoyed the privilege of eating outside, behind the restaurant, with Marvin.

They sat on the retaining wall overlooking the river. The waitress would let Marvin know when he was needed to fill an order.

"Paul. You look great. What did you do to yourself?"

Paul debated with himself as to whether to fess up his affair with Megan. He decided to say nothing about it. He felt protective of Megan's reputation; at least sensitive to her possible preference to not being outed with an eighteen-year-old.

"Just trying to clean up," he replied. He told Marvin about his fine river run to Clancy and they agreed to meet on the river on Marvin's next day off.

It was late afternoon when he got back to his campsite. He was surprised that Megan's truck was still not there and the closed sign was on the door. He loaded the fixings for their late supper and he decided to check on Megan by driving up to her trailer. There was no sign of her or the truck. Paul went home and bedded down wondering if her absence had anything to do with their wild day and night of lovemaking. He still felt her on his private parts. He was partly sore and partly buzzed by their multiple contacts. He assumed his sleep position with a sigh and drifted off thinking about sleeping in a real bed. With Megan.

PART 3

FRIDAY/SATURDAY, MAY 23 AND 24, 1997

Megan did not appear on Friday morning and that left Paul restless and out of sorts. He made his morning toilet and cleaned the rest room in his usual way.

When 9 AM passed he decided to open the kitchen and prep for her eventual arrival. It was intended as a favor. The Friday, semi-weekly, food delivery was a slight problem. Megan was a c.o.d. customer. The only funds available were the $50.00 change in the cash register. So he paid cash out of his own pocket and got a receipt. They'd need the stuff for the weekend rush.

Paul guessed he should call the police to see if there had been an accident. Surely, he thought, Megan would find a way to leave him a message if it were only a simple delay.

He closed early and drove to the COC motel pay phone. He dialed 911 and announced to the flat male voice answering, "What is your emergency?"

"Sir. This is Paul Hunter. I work for Megan Smith who owns the Barbecue Shack Restaurant. She's been away for 3 days and I'm worried that she may have had an accident."

"Hold one," the voice commanded. After a short silence the voice said, "Mr. Hunter. We can check that for you but can you come down to the station and give us some ID and give details in a report?"

"Yes sir. I'll come now. I'm calling from the pay phone at the Caverns Outdoor Center."

"Could I please have your address and telephone number?'

Paul answered, "I'm camping near the Barbecue Shack. But I don't have a phone number."

The police sergeant wore a nametag announcing that his name was Clancy. Paul introduced himself and was told "We have a report of a bad single-vehicle accident Wednesday night in Asheville, involving a Megan Smith of Clancy, Georgia. 33-years old. She was driving a Ford pickup truck and was admitted to Mission Hospital in Asheville. Sorry. That's all I can tell you. We have no information about her injuries. Is she a good friend?"

"She's been my boss for two years and yes we are friends.

"Officer Clancy. My brother lives in Asheville. Would you have a phone here so that I can call him? Collect?"

Paul was given a phone and told not to worry about the charges. He called Mitch and gave him a quick rundown. “Mitch. Could you meet me there in 2 hours? Say about nine. At the front Desk.”

“Paul. Molly and I will be there. Drive carefully.”

The hospital’s main lobby was a cheerful and well illuminated. Mitch and Molly were waiting for him. Looking worried.

The receptionist looked up Megan on her computer and turned to a second receptionist with a question, “Excuse me honey. What does this mean?”

The second receptionist wheeled over on her chair, looked at the screen for a moment and said to Paul, “Megan Smith has been transferred to another location. She went, this morning, to the Willis Rehabilitation Campus. It’s not far but you should drive.” She gave Paul a map.

“Cripes Mitch. I’m worried.”

Molly looked at him with tears in her eyes. “Paul. Were you close to this woman?’

“Yes. Very. She’s my boss and I’ve been trying to take care of the Barbecue Shack for her. Let’s go now? Can we drive together?”

The rehab hospital was sited on a hill nearby and they had a little difficulty navigating to the driveway. The receptionist gave them a room number and an encouraging smile. “Talk to her nurse if you have any questions.”

Thirty minutes later they sat on a bench in shock. “Oh my God guys. I’m sick.”

They were all somber faced and near tears.

Megan had been horribly broken in a high-speed accident on I-40 Wednesday night. She had head and spinal injuries. She was unconscious but her eyes were half open and uncomprehending. Her face was twisted in a grimace.

The nurse was kind but offered little hope or information. "I can only give information to immediate family members. You'll have to talk to the doctor."

They fared little better with the information specialist at the front of the hospital. "You are her first visitors. We have no information on her other than her address and the police investigating the accident are looking for relatives.

"Do you know her next of kin or any relative we can inform of her condition?" Paul could not help but he promised to get in touch with the Asheville police in the morning. It was after midnight - too late to consider driving home, so he bunked with Mitch and Molly. It was the worst night of his life.

The awful night was followed by a terrible morning. He started by tracking down Megan's doctor – the physician on duty that is. Dr. Singh. Megan was not a private patient.

"Paul. I understand that you are the only visitor she's had and admin is trying to find her next of kin to consult with them on her treatment plan.

"I can only tell you that her condition is grave and she might not survive."

Paul eyes teared up.

"I'm not saying that she can't recover. We will do everything we can but we must be honest with each other. Yes?"

Paul nodded. “Thank you doctor. Can you put my name down to call if there is any change?”

Doctor Singh agreed and Paul gave him Mitch’s telephone number. Paul slept on Mitch and Molly’s couch that night having nightmares involving a terrible automobile accident in slow motion. He was at the wheel but could not steer. It was wintertime and he was fighting for control of the car on an endless slick of black ice.

SUNDAY, MAY 24, 1997

Sunday morning he made his way back to the hospital to find no change in Megan. He assured the nurse that he would be looking for a family member and drove to the Barbecue Shack pondering what to do?

He saw several options including shutting the business until others, he did not know who, decided how to proceed. He could keep the place picked up. He would put a Temporary Closed sign in the window. Or maybe he could continue to camp by the river and paddle the summer away, trying to get trips as a standby guide. That meant showing up at the COC rafting office in the mornings and waiting around.

The standby crew did not get paid unless they caught a trip and they actually worked a bit around the rafting area stacking, deflating and cleaning rafts and gear. This was a kind of suck-up procedure where they hoped to get favorable notice from the regular rafting guides and supervisors. It could be very dull and unrewarding for a rookie this time of year.

Paul thought long and hard on the drive back to Clancy. He thought that just pocketing the money and letting things slide might put him in jeopardy of being declared a thief of the business. He wanted to erase his history of stealing and become a better man than he was a kid. He didn't like the idea of standing by while the food went bad and vandals discovered opportunities to spoil her property.

He finally decided to keep the place open for Megan and make sure that it suffered no damage from neglect. But for how long? And to what ultimate end? He would have to go through her stuff to find leads to her friends and family information.

One thing he did not feel was a suitable option was just folding his tent and stealing back to Huntsville with this terrible calamity hanging over Megan.

MEMORIAL DAY, MAY 26, 1997

Paul rose early and opened the restaurant at the usual time. The 3rd day of the Memorial Day weekend was busy but uneventful.

After closing the Shack, he went to Megan's trailer and unlocked it using the spare key he found hanging from a nail she'd driven into the side of the deck. Somehow he knew it would be hanging there on the deck he had built for her a year earlier. He walked the path to her pole-mounted mailbox and found a week's accumulation. He reckoned that the mailman must think she was away.

The floor was dry but the air smelled a little musty with a slight overlay of sex. The bed was made and there were no dishes in the sink. Megan was neat. Like me, he thought. He opened all the windows. There was a screen door in front and he left this open as well. The late spring day freshness soon aired the place out.

He looked at the mail hoping for clues. "Megan. Who are you? Where is your family?" he muttered.

The electric bill, the phone bill and a variety of advertisements did not tell him what he needed to know. There were no long distance calls on the bill.

He made a cup of coffee and found nothing good to eat in the refrigerator. There were a number of leftover bits and pieces and a brownish hunk of lettuce. He tossed it all.

Business was slow and Marvin sat with him as he devoured a steak and fries. Marvin looked natural in his cook's hat and white tee. He sat at ease with his arm resting on the back of the booth and a twinkle in his eye.

"We on for tomorrow bud?"

"Naw Marvin. I can't make it. Something's come up."

Marvin's jaw dropped as Paul related Megan's sad story.

"So I'm going to be working at the shack every day until she's out of the woods."

"I'll stop by and look in on you. If you need help I'll ask Susan to find someone to give you a day off when you need it." Susan, Marvin's wife, was something of a hippie as were many in the COC orbit. She was a food service pro but now somewhat limited by the need to care for their 3-year old son.

"We have lots of friends who could use work."

"Thanks Marvin." Paul's eyes suddenly leaked tears. "Oh God. She's so hurt."

Paul called his parents for advice. "I want to help her but I'm worried that someone might claim that I'm stealing her business Mom?

"What should I do?"

Paul honey. I can see that this is very upsetting for you. I've had a lot of business experience over the years but this is a first for me. How about I call my cousin Fred, the lawyer, and ask his opinion? Get back to me tomorrow and we can talk again."

When he called her again his mother said, "Be careful. Keep records. Stash the money in a bank account and make deposits for each day's receipts. You're doing all right, but you'll have to try harder to find her relatives. Fred said so too. Find her family. Talk to a local lawyer."

MONDAY, JUNE 2, 1997

The days slid by. Paul's doubts and fears about his own position began to intrude on his concern for Megan. She lay in a coma, unattended by family. Paul was weary of working 6 days a week. He went to Asheville once each week to check on Megan. Her facial bruises healed but she lay slack jawed and unresponsive. Dr. Singh still expressed hope but Paul was discouraged

Bills began to pile up on the trailer's kitchen counter. There was a mortgage notice in the mail, an electric bill and many others that demanded attention. His least favorite bill was the demand for a sales tax report. The notice required a weekly payment and Paul felt that he had to act fast.

He had not found her checkbook or purse. He assumed that they were in her vehicle. He'd have to find how to claim her stuff.

Paul had searched her trailer and the nooks and crannies of the restaurant. There were no clues about her family or friends. Maybe, he thought, he'd get more information from her bank statement when it came.

Paul was now sleeping in Megan's bed. His tent and gear were neatly packed in the back of his truck.

One of his many concerns was the pile of cash that he was accumulating. He wrote each day's cash register total on a lined pad and noted all expenses that he paid. As the season approached business grew stronger. He was taking in over $2,500.00 a week and paying the food truck driver about 20 percent. There were few other cash expenses but the bills piling up in the trailer were getting serious. He had over $7,000.00 in a bag under the front seat of his truck.

"Marvin. I've gotta have a regular day off. Can you find someone who'd be trustworthy to handle the Shack for me on Wednesdays? I need someone who knows about foodservice. I can pay $8.00 an hour plus the tip jar."

"Sure. Easy. How about me?" Marvin grinned at him. "Susan wants me to work longer hours at COC but I can do this for you for a while. We'll be looking - Susan and me that is - for someone who can spell you as much as you need. The whole season if necessary."

"I'll need to show you what to do first. Could you make it Tuesday and Wednesday this week?"

WEDNESDAY, JUNE 11, 1997

Paul lay in Megan's bed, sleeping in when he got the idea. He picked up the telephone and looked at the caller ID list. There had been several incoming calls from the same number in the 828 area code. He hit the redial button

Somewhere a phone rang and a pleasant woman's voice exclaimed, "Megan! Where the hell have you been girl?"

"Er… Hi. It's not Megan. My name is Paul Hunter and I work for Megan. I just hit the redial on her phone and you answered.

"Are you a friend of Megan's?"

"This is Martha Nelson. Yes. I have been calling her for days but the phone doesn't answer. Is she there?"

There was a silence on the line as Paul began telling her about Megan's accident.

"So I need to find a family member to take charge at the hospital and take over her business.

"I'm going to be in Asheville late tomorrow afternoon. Would you be able to meet me at the rehab center? We could visit her and then compare notes about how to contact her family."

"Yes. But I might not be able to help much. What time?" Martha thanked him for calling.

Paul opened a bank account in his own name the next day with a single deposit of $6.000.00. He got a temporary checkbook using Megan's mailing address. He visited the offices of the power and gas companies to make payments with his new checks. No one seemed to notice or care about the situation.

The agent at the tax office wasn't so easy. Paul had found the sales tax reporting forms and filled in the appropriate information. He knew that there was a tax office in Clancy.

The man asked about Megan and Paul gave him a complete answer.

"You'll have to fill out an application for yourself for the weeks you are paying. We'll need to get some more information about Miss. Smith's situation because there are 2 weeks missing."

The tax application troubled him but he sat and completed it in the office. He had to use his social security number and register as a new business. There was a section where he could narrate details pertaining to the previous owner of the business. He wrote that: I am just the present operator of the Barbecue Shack. The owner, Megan Smith, has been in a coma in the Asheville Rehab center since May 15, 1997. I intend to keep the business going until she returns and will be responsible for collection and reporting of sales and taxes.

He later told Marvin and his wife Susan, "That was gnarly. I was scared that they'd bust me for something. In the end the guy said that he was glad that I'd come in before a situation developed. I guess Georgia really needs its sales taxes."

He intended to pay the mortgage and some other necessary bills by mail as soon as he got back to the trailer.

Martha Nelson was a tiny woman. A thirtyish, slim and black haired bundle of energy. She bustled into the waiting room and immediately spotted Paul.

"Thank you so much for calling me. Megan is a dear friend. We met at an art class at UNCA a couple of years ago. Usually we meet for drinks, dinner and a movie. I'm single. I work as a nurse at Memorial Hospital. Tell me more about you."

Paul recited his history with Megan and concluded, "I've known her since last year. We've become great friends and I don't want to see all her hard work destroyed by neglect. So I've kept the Barbecue Shack open. I've been paying the bills and taxes and my salary out of the store's income. Keeping the records and so forth."

He hesitated, a little embarrassed..."I'm living in Megan's trailer. Going through her things to find a relative. I only know that there is an ex-husband and a brother she doesn't talk to... I mean get along with."

"Well Paul. I'm in the same boat. I know the ex's name was Robert Turner and he lived in Los Angeles. Her brother's first name is Marty and he's in Chicago. I guess the name is really Martin Smith.

"I don't envy your position. We have a little circle of friends for our girls-night-out. I'll talk it up with them.

"Let's go see her."

Megan was the same. She seemed a little smaller than last week. It seemed that she might be losing weight despite her feeding and therapy programs. They stayed and spoke to her and stroked her arms. They were both crying when it was time to go.

"Paul. I tried to call her so many times. Why don't you get a good answering machine to monitor the telephone? Maybe someone will call."

They hugged, sharing their sorrow.

"Molly," Paul said at dinner. I've bought an answering machine for Megan's phone. I don't want to chance missing any more calls. Would you record the answering message for me? I don't want a male voice.

After a bit of practice they recorded a minimalist message in Molly's sweetest voice; "Megan's phone. Leave a message.

WEDNESDAY, JUNE 18, 1997

Paul's hair was long enough for a ponytail. The long hair and beard were not formulated in his mind as a policy or deliberate statement. It was the easy way to get through the days.

The saga continued without change until the county health inspector arrived. She was Miss. C. White, according to her nametag. Fortunately she came on a day that Paul was there.

He followed her around like a puppy while she looked into every nook and cranny with a flashlight in one gloved hand and a clipboard in the other. She made notes and checked squares on her form.

"Where is the thermometer in this reefer?" she said, indicating the under-the-counter refrigerator where coleslaw, uncooked hot dogs and miscellaneous groceries were kept.

"Uh. Sorry. I don't know." He got on his knees and stuck his head in the cooler. He saw the thermometer hanging from a wire shelf and proudly brought it out.

She smiled. "Very good. And I need your grease pump-out record."

He shrugged his shoulders and gave her a rueful look. "Sorry. I don't know where it is."

Miss White gave him a hint. "Megan usually has it under the cash register."

Sure enough. There was a pick-up record indicating that a company that specialized in recycling the nasty stuff had emptied the grease trap on the 16th of May. He saw that there was another envelope under the register. He left it there while she finished her inspection.

"Very good inspection," she said. "But there is one more thing. I need to see your health education certificate or schedule you for a class at the County health Department." He signed up for the class scheduled for the next Monday morning at 8 AM.

Miss White left him a certificate indicating an "A" rating of 92. He had lost points for not having his certificate of training.

He looked at the envelope under the register as she left. It contained sales tax reports for the two missing weeks with a single check attached for the total amount. He saw that she banked with First National and he resolved to hand deliver the reports as soon as possible. He checked one small worry off his plate.

That same day, the mailman left the bank statement along with a few bills and ads.

He popped the statement open and studied the checks she'd written. There were no surprises. Her balance was a $1,050.00 and he guessed that the check for the sales tax would the only one outstanding.

Paul had a stack of unpaid bills including:

- The mortgage for both the trailer and the restaurant property
- Automobile insurance due to Geico
- Business liability Insurance
- Car payment
- Sears Department Store
- JC Penny. (This had a small credit balance)
- The county annual business license renewal
- The Power and Light Company
- Gas company for both the trailer and restaurant tanks
- Magazine subscriptions
- Chamber of commerce dues

He wrote checks for utility bills and others that seemed essential for both the residence and business. He wrote the checks from his new account and prepared the envelopes for mailing as he had seen his mother do every month.

Finding the tax forms under the cash register inspired him to search the trailer again, even though he had worked hard at it before. He checked under the mattress, in the freezer, in the cups and bowls in the kitchen and in the pans under the sink. He looked under the rugs behind pictures.

It was almost midnight when he found Megan's address book in the couch. It was way down under the cushions. He thought it might have fallen there when they made love.

There were about 20 names. Some had area codes and some had addresses. Some were cryptic - just initials or numbers without a name.

MONDAY JUNE 30, 1997

This was Paul's 6th week of despair. Megan seemed to be failing and Dr. Singh gave him little hope. He had exhausted Megan's address book and had no leads to her ex-husband or brother. The working numbers were all businesses and the people answering could or would not give him much information about their business with Megan. There were a few disconnected numbers.

He was banking the receipts from the Shack. They increased a little every week and the last weekend in June was very busy. Every day would be busy in the upcoming month of July and the weekends were already brutal. Kids were out of school and families prowled the area looking for mountain recreation and roadside barbecue.

Paul kept the restaurant going for 6 weeks before he threw in the towel. He was tired of working 7 days a week and the constant worry about his uncertain position. And he opened a notice from Geico including a check for $15,000.00 payable to Megan and The First National Bank. It was to pay off the loan and compensate Megan for the total loss of her truck. He closed at noon and headed for town with a bagful of Megan's bills, cash register receipts and all the miscellaneous paperwork he had collected.

Throwing in the towel meant consulting with the town's biggest law office, Johns and Johns. The firm occupied a Victorian mansion on Main Street. The dated building was perfectly maintained and looked as good as new. His appointment was for one o'clock.

Paul wore a clean outfit consisting of jeans and a shirt with a collar. This was the best he could do for this occasion. He was conscious of wrinkles in his shirt and scuffs on his boots.

The elderly receptionist asked him to have a seat in the waiting room. It was nicely furnished and Paul felt slightly intimidated. She offered him coffee or water but he politely declined.

After a time an elderly man entered the room and said "Hello."

He was nattily dressed wearing bright red suspenders with a matching tie over a very white shirt.

He introduced himself. "Johnny Johns," he said offering a firm handshake. "Step this way young man so we can talk in my office." He led the way into the back of the office suite. It was a somber place with antique furniture and expensive looking pictures on the walls.

The lawyer sat in a leather chair on the client side of the desk and motioned Paul to sit in a matching chair. "How can I help you today?" he asked kindly.

Paul was surprised to be sitting on the same side as the desk with Attorney Johns. It was a down to earth way to conduct business.

"Well sir. I've gotten myself into a situation. I need advice, but before I ask my questions I should tell you I'm willing to pay for your time. Excuse me for asking but I need to know how much you'll charge. I'm embarrassed to ask so bluntly but I feel a need to know." Paul sat on the edge of his chair.

"Good question Mr. Hunter. May I call you Paul?"

"Yes sir," said Paul venturing a smile.

"Paul. Call me Johnny. Everyone does. If you say Johns people won't know whom you're talking about.

"Let me tell you that I've been in business here in Clancy for over 30 years with my late brother George. I never charge for an initial consultation.

"If I agree to help you I'll probably charge $75.00 per hour billed in 15 minute increments. If it is a criminal matter I'll need to be paid in advance. So you see I'm not cheap but my advice is usually pretty good." He winked at Paul in an avuncular manner and sat attentively in his chair, looking directly at Paul in a friendly manner.

"That will be fine sir." He began to tell Johnny the story of Megan. He told him everything except that they were having a relationship. "I've been staying in her trailer to better look after things but I'm very uneasy that I'm getting into trouble.

"My uncle who's a lawyer in Alabama told my mom that I should just pack up and leave. She told me to leave the keys with the police in Clancy and make sure they have the whole story.

"But here's what I'm worried about. If I just leave someone might break into her house and trash it. Probably the business too and she'll have nothing when she gets better. I mean if she gets better." Paul was very emotional and close to crying as he concluded his recital.

Johnny was quiet for a moment. He leaned toward Paul and said, "Paul. I'm sorry to learn of these circumstances. Do you want to take over the business?"

"No sir… I mean Johnny. Megan's my friend and I just want to have her come back to work and tell me what to do."

"How old are you Paul?"

"Nineteen sir… er, Johnny."

"Paul, were you intimate with Megan?"

Paul hesitated trying to find the right words. "She was my employer and landlord since last summer. We were very good friends but we made love the night before she had her crash. She was older than me but we had just started. We were supposed to have dinner when she returned."

Johnny did not seem to pass judgment. His face remained alert and interested,

"What is your education and work experience?"

Paul told him about his recent graduation from high school and working construction for his dad. "Oh yeah. I forgot. I got a health department certificate for taking a sanitation lecture and test and I'm an accredited raft guide for Caverns Outdoor Center. I took the 7-day course."

Johnny nodded. "Paul, based on what you have shared with me, you haven't done anything wrong. Yet.

"You could step over the line if you continue after Megan passes, if indeed she does." Johnny paused, rose and crossed the room. He handed Paul a tissue.

Paul wiped his eyes and blew his nose. "Thanks Johnny. This is scary stuff for me."

"Paul. I will be willing to help you in this matter for my usual fees that can be paid as we go along. It's really not too complicated but it will take some time. At $75.00 per hour I'm guessing that you may be looking at a bill for one or two thousand dollars plus modest court filing fees.

"I see you as a guardian of Megan's assets until she gets back or dies. From what you tell me her condition is deteriorating. You have done her heirs, should there be any, your community, and the state of Georgia no harm. Indeed, you are the good guy."

Paul smiled to hear this. "Johnny. How do you mean her guardian?"

"I believe that we could apply to the Clancy County Superior Court to appoint you as a guardian of her real property, and that would include the business. Paul. I like the way you have conducted yourself. Since you are young and inexperienced I would be willing to join you in the effort.

"Paul. I'm on the verge of retirement. I have no need of fees. I'll be closing this office at the end of the month – this would be one of my projects in retirement. I'll go easy on the fees, but we will need to use an investigator. That may be our main expense.

"As a part of conserving her property and business affairs she would need to become a ward of the court and, should she pass, we would need to take steps to not only locate her family but liquidate her business and sell the real estate.

"Should you be willing to continue to work for Megan and her heirs, when and if we find them, I'd expect you to remain in place for a period of time.

"Today is the last day of June. If you will agree to stay on, I'll need a few days to file the petition. My fee for that will be $200.00 but I'll need a check from you for $1,000.00.

"I also need to investigate you. I want to be sure that you are who you told me you are. I'll need personal references.

"We'll have to get a statement from this Dr. Singh in Asheville. I'll do the legwork on all of these matters, but we need to act swiftly at this time to be sure that we can get the blessings of the court on your actions.

"Do you want to continue Paul?"

Johnny seemed to shift into another mode as he laid out a plan of action for Paul. His demeanor was very friendly and supportive. But he seemed to become younger and more animated as he spoke.

"Johnny. I need to talk to my mom to get her advice. Is there a phone that I could use?

"Paul. You have just revealed yourself as an intelligent as well as a kind man. Use the phone in the conference room if you like and I'll make a few phone calls on this. No fee yet. But I want to get a few things lined up." He showed Paul into an adjacent room with a library table surrounded by 6 comfortable chairs on wheels. There was a large picture window and lots of light.

There was a stack of yellow pads and pens on the table and a telephone with several lines indicated by buttons. He pushed a button and punched in his mother's number.

Paul's mother heard him out and concurred that he needed Johnny John's help. He made a note of his second cousin's address and phone number in Birmingham to use him as a reference.

"Good luck honey. I know that you are doing the right thing."

Paul walked back to Johnny's office and waited at the door for Johnny to put the phone down. Johnny's last words into the receiver were, "Thank you sweetie. I'll wait here for your phone call."

He looked up at Paul, smiled, and gestured for him to be seated. Johnny stayed on the working side of the desk this time.

"What did your mom say Paul?"

"She told me to stay as long as I needed and to say thank you for helping me Johnny.

"And I need to show you this check and ask you what should I do with it?"

Johnny looked at the $15,000.00 check and glanced at the form letter from GEICO. "We'll just attach this to the file for now. We may need to negotiate with the insurance company after looking at the vehicle, the loan papers and the black book. We'll talk about this later. The main thing is to get you settled.

"Well then. Let's you and I get moving. We have a lot to do. My investigator's name is Carmen Cabrera. She is a retired Florida State Highway Patrol officer. She is right now heading for the Barbecue Shack to make sure that it is as you say it is. I hope she likes the food," he chuckled.

"I'm sure she will if she likes to eat. The slaw is made fresh and the pork is smoked on a daily basis. The only thing we freeze is the bread so that it stays as fresh as the day it's baked. Please let me know what she has to say. My friend Susan Reed is running the show today. She and her husband Marvin take turns helping me so that I can get days off to go to Asheville every week."

"I see. Are they legal employees?"

"Yes and no. But I get the point. I'll get their Social Security numbers right away and withhold taxes. Is that what you mean?"

"Yes Paul. We are about to enter the real world. We need to dot our 'I's and cross our 'T's.

"Paul. We have a great deal to do if we are to succeed in our efforts right away. By Wednesday I expect to have the court appoint you and me as guardians of Megan's property. Friday is the 4th of July weekend and the court will begin its vacation recess for 4 weeks. I want you to go to the office of Smith and Company. They are accountants. Just down the street. I have already spoken to them and they will help you apply for an Employers Identification Number, by phone. They'll give you the forms you need to legalize Marvin, Susan and yourself as employees.

"Paul. Please write your name, Social Security Number, your address and telephone numbers and the names and contact numbers for as many references as you can. Please give me your brother's and parent's contact information too.

"I'll need you to return to my office at ten o'clock Wednesday morning and be prepared to go to court with me. My secretary has already made an appointment with the judge and the county attorney for a hearing on the matter at noon.

Johnny questioned Paul closely about the income from the Shack and the expenses of both the business and Megan personally. He got all the details about how Paul handled the cash register tapes, expenses and deposits.

Paul took the time to write all that Johnny requested on a lined pad. He gave his second cousin Fred McDowell, the lawyer, Marvin Redman, his friend, and his high school Lit teacher as references. He gave the list to Johnny with a personal check for $1,000.00. He felt that he was doing it for Megan and, for the first time in weeks, enjoyed confidence in his actions. He felt like he'd been in a state of uncertainty since he said goodbye to a healthy Megan.

"I want you to get a good start in the right direction. Please shave, get a haircut and wear a jacket and tie. You'll clean up fine my boy!"

Smith and Company's offices were not as elegant as Johns and Johns. Accountant Regan Smith was alone and on the phone as Paul entered with his paper bag of records.

Smith had a ruddy face. He was a white haired, handsome guy in his fifties and he spoke with a musical, high-pitched voice. "Yes. Yes. No." He smiled and motioned for Paul to be seated on the other side of his cluttered desk. "Hold on a moment please."

"Paul. Hi I'm Regan. I'm on the phone getting your Employers Identification Number from the IRS.

What is your Social Security number and address?" He paused for a moment, and then said, "Paul Hunter? Do you have a middle initial?"

Paul answered his questions and presently Regan said goodbye and put the phone down.

"Johnny briefed me on your situation. I'm sorry about Ms. Smith. I don't know her by the way. We're probably not related.

"Paul. I told Johnny that I would not charge you for today's work. He briefed me on your situation. I've gotten you an EIN and have here a file of information of your responsibilities as an employer relating to Workman's Compensation Insurance and Georgia State Income tax.

Go through this stuff and come back to me after your court date on Wednesday and I'll answer any questions you have. Just read it all over. A lot of it is self-explanatory." He handed Paul a manila file folder containing a neat stack of pages.

"Thank you. How do you charge for your services?"

"Good question. It depends on how much work I have to do. In the case of your business I would guess $50.00 per month plus $200.00 next spring if you want me to do your taxes. Sound Good?"

"Yeah. I mm…mean yes sir." They both laughed.

Since it was too late to go the distance to Asheville, and because he had not made advance arrangements with Mitch and Molly, he decided to shop for clothes and get a haircut. There was a Walmart in Clayton, Georgia but the drive put him off.

Solomon's Menswear on Main Street was his best and only choice. There was a 'Summer Madness' sale. He left the store, under the kindly eye of Sol Solomon, with a complete 'Go-To- Court' outfit; chino pants, blue short-sleeve shirt, belt, black knit tie and blue blazer. He bought black loafers and several pairs of socks at the neighboring Shoe Heaven. These were all cash transactions.

Then to the barbershop. The barber remembered his name from his first visit. "Say Paul. I'm going to have to use the electric shaver on you before I can give you a regular shave."

"No problem. Thanks for taking me on." Afterwards the air felt cooler on his face.

"Marvin. I need a big favor from you and Susan."

"Sure bud. What is it?" Marvin was just finishing his daily cleanup work. He didn't comment on the change in Paul's look. He was a patient man and he was sure Paul would explain.

"Actually 2 things. I want to keep our business; I mean Megan's business, confidential. I don't want folks around here or at COC to know what I'm up to."

"Why Paul. You're doing good things. I'd be proud if I were you."

"Yeah. I don't disagree but I'm going to court Wednesday to ask to become Megan's Legal Guardian along with lawyer Johnny Johns. I figure that this won't last long. I don't think Megan is going to make it. By the way, Johnny made me shave and get a haircut."

Paul was frankly crying and, to his surprise, he saw that Marvin was crying too. Marvin put down his dishtowel and gave Paul a hug. "I know it's tough bud. We'll do what we can to help."

"The thing is that I'm 18-years old and I feel way in over my head. I don't want people to think I'm some smart guy. I want to fit in and just be a working stiff. Maybe at COC next year. However long this lasts I want it to end clean and not follow me around as a part of my rep. Ya know?"

"I see what you mean. I'll talk to Susan and we'll not gossip about you. I promise. We haven't said much so far because I don't want my boss to know that we're working for the competition, although she probably already knows. Cornelia Johnson is a smart lady and there's not much that gets by her.

"Thanks Marvin. And there's something else. I need to back track on our deal here. I want to give you and Susan a 10% raise in pay but, in return, you have to go on the books and I need to start paying you by check and deducting Social Security from your checks. I'm not exactly sure how that works but I'll find out Wednesday. Okay?"

"Yes, sure. We'll be glad to cooperate. Just figure it out and let us know."

That night he settled down to read through employer and employee manuals, state and federal income tax forms, workman compensation rules and a handful of forms. He understood them pretty well. Even at the low rates of pay for Marvin, Susan and himself, he would have to deduct taxes, account for them and pay them to the appropriate authorities. He wondered how Megan had avoided all this bother. He guessed she was a rogue, bootleg business operating outside the system. He imagined the worry this must have cost her over the 3 years she'd told him she'd been in business.

He arrived at Johnny's office at 10 AM on Wednesday morning. The secretary invited him to sit in the conference room. She gave him a cup of coffee and some heavy reading material. “Johnny will be here in a few minutes.”

The main document was a petition to the Superior Court of Clancy County to appoint him and Johnny as Guardians. It was a beautifully typed and bound document. It proved to be an interesting read for him. He was impressed by the amount of research and initiative it revealed about Johnny and his team. There was no way the old man could have done all this work on his own.

PETITION FOR THE APPOINTMENT OF A GUARDIAN FOR AN ALLEGED INCAPACITATED ADULT

Clancy County, Georgia

TO THE HONORABLE JUDGE OF THE SUPERIOR COURT:
Roland E. Sequoyah

IN RE: Megan Smith, ALLEGED INCAPACITATED ADULT, And PROPOSED WARD:

1. **Paul Hunter**, friend and employee, whose residence address is 1901 Georgia Route 72, Clancy, Georgia 31955, and **J.P. Johns**, Attorney at law representing Paul Hunter as counsel and advisor for fee, and who is a proposed friend, in absence of family, of the proposed ward, is a resident of Clancy County with offices at 12 Main Street, Clancy Georgia, 31955.

ATTACHED HERETO as page 6 and made a part of this petition is the completed **affidavit** of Mohamed Singh, M.D., a physician licensed to practice medicine in both the states of Georgia and North Carolina. (Megan Smith lies in a coma in the Asheville, North Carolina Rehabilitation center) Dr. Singh has examined the proposed ward within 10 days prior to the filing of this petition.

2. Megan Smith, proposed ward, age 33, (May 1 1964), social security no. XXX XX 2198, is a resident of Clancy County, Georgia has a residence address of 1 Robbins Cove Road, Clancy, Georgia 31955 and is presently located at the Asheville Rehabilitation Center in Asheville, North Carolina, where she lies gravely ill and in a coma since May 22, 1997. (The full S.S. number is in possession of Petitioner J. P Johns)

3. The proposed ward lacks sufficient understanding or capacity to make responsible decisions concerning her person and is incapable of managing her estate, and the property of the proposed ward will be wasted or dissipated unless proper management is provided.

As per the attached notarized statement of Dr. Singh and the North Carolina State Police Report 0522196744, Megan Smith lies in a deep coma resulting from a single car accident in North Carolina in the early morning hours of May 22, 1997; cause unknown. **(Alcohol, drugs and foul play have been ruled out pending final disposition of the case)**

The duration of the incapacity is unknown.

4. There are no known relatives or spouse at this time other than a brother, Martin Smith. His whereabouts is under investigation so that he can be notified of Megan Smith's circumstances.

In accordance with the stature, notice is being given to 2 adult friends of Megan Smith. Copies of their signed response will be provided within 7 days:

1. Martha Nelson (Friend of Megan Smith)
   21 Bowery Street
   Asheville North Carolina
   (828) 555 2121
2. Alice Gordan (Friend of Megan Smith)
   1211 Meyers Court
   Asheville North Carolina
   (828) 555-7676

5. There are no previously appointed representatives from prior proceedings pursuant to Official Code of Georgia Annotated Chapters 37-7, 37-3 or 37-4.

6. All known income and assets of the proposed ward are shown on page 7 attached hereto.

7. The nominated guardians have consented to serve have consented to serve as shown by the consent on page 5 attached hereto.

WHEREFORE, the petitioners pray: that service be perfected as required by law; that pending receipt of any evaluation reports, required by the court, the court order an immediate hearing to determine the need for a guardian for the alleged incapacitated person; and that a guardian of the property be appointed for the alleged incapacitated adult.

PAUL L. HUNTER (SIGNATURE)
J.P. JOHNS (SIGNATURE)

J. P. JOHNS
12 MAIN STREET
CLANCY, GEORGIA 31955

VERIFICATION
GEORGIA, CLANCY COUNTY

Personally appeared before me the undersigned petitioner who, on oath, states that the facts set forth in the foregoing petition are true.

MARSHA GRANT, NOTARY PUBLIC

Sworn to and subscribed before this 2nd day of July 1997

RE: Petition for the appointment of guardian for Megan Smith, an alleged incapacitated adult.

I, PAUL HUNTER, having been nominated as guardian of the property of the above-named alleged incapacitated adult, do hereby consent to serve as such.

Paul Hunter (signature)

I, J.P. JOHNS, having been nominated as guardian of the property of the above-named alleged incapacitated adult, do hereby consent to serve as such.

J.P. JOHNS (signature)

AFFIDAVIT OF PHYSICIAN OR PSYCHOLOGIST
STATE OF GEORGIA, COUNTY OF CLANCY
SUPERIOR COURT OF CLANCY COUNTY

RE: Petition for appointment of a guardian for MEGAN SMITH, an alleged incapacitated adult.

I, being first duly sworn, depose and say that I am a physician licensed to practice under Chapter 34 of Title 43 of the Official Code of Georgia Annotated. My office address is Asheville Rehabilitation Center, 1000 Mars Avenue, Asheville, North Carolina, that I have examined the above-named alleged incapacitated adult on the 1st day of July 1997, **and I have found her to be incapacitated by reason of an automobile**

accident, to the extent that said alleged incapacitated adult lacks sufficient understanding or capacity to make significant responsible decisions concerning her person and property and is incapable of communicating such decisions.

WITNESS MY HAND AND SEAL this 1st day of July 1997.

Mohamed Singh, M.D.

(Signed and Notarized in North Carolina)

INCOME AND ASSETS

Below are listed all of the known income and assets of the proposed ward:

REAL PROPERTY

Parcel- 1 - A Manufactured Home at 1 Grant Cove Road, Clancy, Georgia sitting upon one acre of land. Value undetermined, mortgaged to GMAC with a balance of $95,000.00

Parcel-2 - A one-acre lot at 1901 Georgia Highway 72 occupied by a business known as the Barbecue Shack. Value undetermined and also subject to the mortgage cited above.

It is estimated that he Barbecue Shack produces a net income in excess of $25,000.00 per year. No other income is known at this time.

YEARLY TOTAL OF ALL INCOME is estimated to be in excess $25,000.00.

PERSONAL PROPERTY

Checking account – First Citizens, # 45454555 - Balance - $1,050.00

Savings Account - Unknown

CERTIFICATE OF DEPOSIT - Unknown

BONDS - unknown

STOCKS – unknown

AUTOMOBILE 1995 Ford 150 pickup truck - wrecked. This vehicle has been totaled. GEICO Company has tendered a check of $15,000.00 intended to pay the loan off and compensate Megan Smith for the total value of the vehicle. This amount will be negotiated should the court appoint the petitioners as guardians of Megan Smith's estate and property.

OTHER ITEMS

Furniture and incidental personal property including jewelry, business inventory of the Barbecue Shack and other personalty.

TOTAL PERSONAL PROPERTY - Estimated to be in excess of $25,000.00

TOTAL YEARLY INCOME + TOTAL PERSONAL PROPERTY VALUE Estimated to be in excess of $50,000.00

GEORGIA SUPERIOR COURT OF CLANCY COUNTY

Roland E. Sequoyah Judge of the SUPERIOR Court

APPOINTMENT OF ATTORNEY

It appearing that this Court has not been notified of the retention of counsel by the proposed ward within the prescribed period**, J. P. Johns** is hereby temporarily appointed as attorney for the proposed ward in this matter. This 2nd day of July 1997

Roland Sequoyah Judge of the SUPERIOR Court

The main document had yellow arrow stickers placed where he was to sign. There were several other documents including orders for the judge to sign creating the guardianship. He noted Dr. Sing's notarized affidavit and realized someone had traveled to Asheville to get his signature. He was paying for this work but he found that he liked the way Johnny had taken charge and was getting things done.

Judge Sequoyah was a sturdy man of about 45 years. His black hair and dark features that suggested a Native

American heritage. He, Johnny, Paul and a man named Sam Silvers sat at a conference table in the judge's chambers. Silvers turned out to be the State's Attorney. He was there to represent Megan's interests. "So. What's the real story Johnny," the judge said looking directly at Paul.

Paul was dressed in his new clothes but felt out of place among these dignitaries. The judge was in his shirtsleeves with the cuffs rolled up. He was clearly in charge of this proceeding. The others wore jackets and seemed to know each other well.

"Judge. Young Mr. Hunter here is a hero in my estimation. He fell into a bad situation and conducted himself well." He told the story in as few words as possible and concluded. "So like a true friend he kept the business going and has folded his tent, so to speak, and moved into the trailer to keep it clean and repaired. He has paid Ms. Smith's bills.

In addition to going to the police he consulted me and then with Smith and Company, accountants, out to help him find the correct path to follow. He is current with the sales taxes and has paid utilities and mortgage payments."

The judge looked at Paul and said, "Mr. Hunter. I was very sorry to hear about your friend's accident and dire medical condition. I am going to permit you to continue as you have been but I will require a weekly report to be filed with Sam Silvers and the court detailing both Ms. Smith's condition and the financial situation of both from the business and her personal finances. I don't want to see Mr. Hunter enrich himself but I see the need to pay him appropriately for maintaining this 7 days a week business. I propose to pay him not more than $700.00 a week if that is possible given the nature of the business. I want also to see a proposal for closing it down if it can't support itself when the tourist season is over.

"Do you concur gentlemen?"

The attorneys and Paul all nodded and chorused, "Yes Sir."

"Johnny. Get the paperwork ready now. Okay?"

"Yes sir. It will be here by close of business and I'll make sure that it's all signed off by Mr. Silver first."

It was a one-block walk to Johnny's office from the courthouse. Sam Silver's office was in the courthouse. Silver and Johnny had paused to confer out of Paul's earshot. But he saw that were looking at their watches and setting a time to review the orders that Johnny would generate for the court.

"Paul. How do you feel? Did we do good for Megan?"

"Yes sir Johnny. Thanks to you. I think so. I don't know about the $700.00 per week. It may be a little too much after the season is over. Everything will slow down in the shoulder season."

"Let's not worry about that right now." Johnny said kindly. "Just come to the office and I'll figure out what you need to sign. Most of the forms we use are on the computer now and it doesn't take too long to fill in the blanks and print them."

Paul sat in the waiting room thinking. There were magazines and a newspaper but he ignored them. He wanted time to absorb all that had transpired in the judge's office. Johnny came out after a while and said, "Paul. Take a walk for a few minutes. We'll not need you until 3 o'clock. And then it will just take a few minutes."

Paul, liberated, made his way to Smith's Accounting and found Regan finishing up with a client who nodded politely to Paul as he entered. He sat and waited until the man left.

"Paul. What happened in court today?"

Paul told him that he was going to continue to run the business, try to achieve his paycheck and that he would stop by before the end of each month with cash register tapes, an account of receipts and expenses and checks for taxes.

"Paul. Speaking of checks I would appreciate you paying me now. $100.00 will be enough to get me started. I'll work with you for a while but it is my goal to have you do most the work by yourself and I'll just be your coach. Johnny will tell me what he needs and I'll just bill you as we go along."

They agreed on meeting times and dates; weekly at first. Paul returned to the law office with a determination to be a good client for Smith. He liked him very much and wanted his approval.

Johnny sat Paul at the conference table and presented him with a series of legal papers, some requiring signature and other just a nod of understanding. These were the orders that gave him the legal authority to continue doing what he had already undertaken as an act of friendship for Megan. He just wanted her well and back in charge.

Paul was given a folder containing copies of all the documents relating to the case. It was fat enough to make a thump when he put in on a table.

“Paul. In addition to the things we have just discussed there is that matter of settling with the insurance company. Megan probably had personal items in the car and I want you to take a copy of Judge Sequoyah*'s* order with you and go to the police in Asheville next time you go there and see what you can do. I’m thinking about her purse and wallet mostly but there may be other stuff of help in tracking down a family member.”

A week later Paul brought a sealed cardboard box to Johnny’s office. He wanted them to open it together. Megan’s purse and wallet especially were examined in detail and, sadly, there were no further clues, telephone numbers or addresses.

Business grew stronger each day until the weekdays were indistinguishable from weekends. He really needed the days off that Marvin and Susan gave him. Wednesdays and Thursdays were his days to travel to Asheville and see Megan’s sad situation and gain comfort from Mitch and Molly’s company. He usually spent a night on their couch and returned to the trailer Thursday afternoon to do housework and bookkeeping.

The money worked out just as it had before except that he deposited the excess to Megan’s bank account each week. No one had thought about charging him rent for the trailer or some fine points that developed as he worked the days away

The tip jar, for example, yielded a dividend each day. He saw that the more he interacted with customers the bigger the take. It was a funny thing. It supplied him with a regular side income every day he worked. He always put a few dollar bills and a few quarters first thing in the morning to give customers the idea. He thought of it as 'salting' the jar. Most put in loose change and a few left folding money. He didn't really care because he felt happiest when he smiled and said a friendly hello to everyone. He kept that money to himself.

He took all his meals at work except for his days off. His little scams also involved getting the weekly food delivery to include some extras like cereal, milk, coffee and his favorite brand of baked beans. The food was an efficiency move for him rather that a ploy to save a few dollars a day. He was able to open earlier and stay a little later.

He mailed his mother a check for $500.00 on a weekly basis and accumulated a balance in his personal checking account. His opportunities to get out on the river were limited.

Paul made a few office visits to Johnny and Regan who worked together, from the information Regan extracted from his checkbook and cash register tapes. He prepared his own Sales Tax Reports and Regan made a copy. Regan taught him to make Withholding Tax and Social Security payments to the IRS. The reports were easy enough.

Susan and Marvin didn't care that a little was withheld each week. The tip jar probably made up for their small contributions to the government. He put posters and official notices on the back walls of the Shack advising the employees of their rights and responsibilities.

He saw many new faces each day and a few regulars and friends too. It was not a hard job but it did require good organization and proper prepositioning of all the supplies he needed every day and thorough cleaning always.

He enjoyed working with the food. Turning cabbage into delicious coleslaw and raw pork into savory barbecue was fun.

His bank balances grew quickly even though Regan had him make checks to Megan on a weekly basis. He no longer had to pay the mortgage because Johnny found out that there was a disability clause and no payments were due while she was unable to work. In fact the mortgage company refunded one month's payment and that went straight into Megan's bank. Her account had also grown by an additional $1,500.00 from the automobile insurance policy. Johnny had negotiated a higher payout.

PART 4

SEPTEMBER 5, 1997

Dr. Singh called and said, “Paul. I have sad news for you. Megan did not survive the night. As you know we have no relatives to call. There was an investigator here a few weeks ago and she gave me the hint that you are being appointed as Megan’s guardian. Is this true?”

“Yes sir. Thank you for calling… I’ve been bracing myself for this.

“What is the situation now? I mean about her body?

“Paul, as you probably know from her driver’s license Megan chose to be an organ donor. Unless someone comes forward to object, her body will go immediately to the state coroner and there it will be decided what to do with her remains. The state of North Carolina will incur expenses that will probably be dismissed due to the complexity of collecting. There will be a large hospital bill that may be filed against her estate in Georgia. You'll need legal counsel if you have an interest in these matters.

"I wish I could tell you more but matters are now out of the hospital's hands and I can only say that I'm sorry that we couldn't save her."

Paul sniffled a goodbye and thank you. He felt defeated. He felt he had failed Megan utterly.

Mitch and Molly took over. They sat down with Paul in their living room. "Paul. This is an intervention. We'd like to ask the hospital chaplain if they could help us conduct a service for Megan. We never knew her but we feel like friends and family. We want to say goodbye to her in a proper way."

Phone calls were made that resulted in a solemn service conducted in the chapel on the Tuesday following her death. Paul was surprised that over two-dozen people attended. She had several friends in Asheville and there were members of the hospital staff.

Paul rode to the occasion in a COC van with 9 people from COC and Clancy including the judge, Johnny, Regan and their wives. Marvin and Susan brought their child. He had arranged for and driven the vehicle. Carmen, Johnny's investigator was there and he recognized a number of Megan's nurses. He was touched by their attendance.

A party of 14 went to a downtown tavern that had been frequented by Megan and her friends and had a meal. Mitch and Molly had been right – the activity and memorial service made Paul feel better about things– Megan had a good sendoff.

"Paul. We must carry on as the court dictates and as the laws of North Carolina and Georgia dictate. I believe that it will be in the best interest of Megan's estate if you will continue on for a short while until we get instructions from the court. I believe that it will order Megan's property liquidated. As to the business, I think it can be sold quickly. There are brokers who deal in the buying and selling of businesses. Thanks to you; Megan has a valuable business that might well be continued under a new owner.

"Do you have any interest in acquiring the business?"

"No Johnny. It's not that I don't like it but if I could buy it, the Shack would own me. Remember I'm only nineteen and I haven't figured my life course out yet." Paul was embarrassed to admit this but he did not have a real plan beyond getting a job with COC for a season to be able to continue playing on the river.

Many of his river friends were a good bit older but they seemed content to enjoy nature's bounty and each other's company without much concern about the future. He admired that about them but thought that something important would catch his interest one day.

FRIDAY, SEPTEMBER 12, 1997

Judge Sequoyah, Johnny, Paul and State Attorney Sam Silvers sat in the judge's conference room again. They were a somber group gathered to decide the fate of Megan Smith's property and business.

"Gentlemen," the judge said in a gravelly voice, "The law dictates what we do now." It seemed to Paul that he was getting a lecture, the same lecture Johnny had given him. "We must act with deliberate speed to liquidate the deceased's assets and that means selling her business and her real estate. Are we agreed?"

All nodded. "Therefore Johnny you will produce documentation, and you Sam will approve or amend it as necessary until complete agreement is reached."

The judge turned to Paul. "Mr. Hunter. It is my understanding that you will occupy the real estate and run the business as a conservation manner, as you have been, until a buyer is found."

"Yes judge." Paul was very nervous. "I'll do the best I can."

"I understand that you are young sir, but I have trust in the fact that Mr. Smith is partnering you and that you will work under his supervision.

"Mr. Silverman. I expect you and Mr. Smith will be able to work this all out together." Silverman nodded. They all rose as the judge stood and everyone shook hands.

Judge Sequoyah held Paul's hand a moment longer than he did the lawyers and said quietly, "Megan would thank you too sir. I thank you for being a stand up guy."

FRIDAY, SEPTEMBER 19, 1997

Johnny was a man of action. Paul was at the Shack window serving lunch on this quiet day when Johnny and a couple showed up just before noon.

Paul had quit shaving again and would grow a beard and long hair by his birthday in December. Today he looked a little windblown and had a heavy five o'clock shadow on his chin and cheeks.

Johnny introduced them as Paula Pruitt from Atlanta, the New Horizons Business Brokers owner, and her client Jerry Marks who was very interested in buying an income property in a rural mountain area.

Paul thought he recognized Jerry as a recent face in the service window. Perhaps he had previewed the place on his own.

"Paul." Johnny addressed him. "Could you please show Paula and Jerry around and then hang a closed sign for the afternoon. We could either eat here, at that restaurant at COC, or bring some food to the trailer. What do you say?"

"Sure Johnny. It's a 'break-even' kind of day and I didn't do much prep. I'll show them around and then pack us a lunch to eat at home… I mean at Megan's."

"How do you do Jerry? Are you from Atlanta?"

Jerry gave Paul a very hard handshake and a rather unfriendly glare, as if they were unfriendly opponents. "No. Miami. How about you?"

""Huntsville." Paul did not embellish. "Come on I'll give you a tour."

"Mind if I tag along?" Paula asked.

"Sure. No worries. There's not much to show." The three explored the property while Johnny sat comfortably at a picnic table. Since it was such a basic enterprise, few questions were asked. Jerry seemed very interested in the exposure to the river and remarked that there wasn't much signage.

"Jerry. There are virtually no signs on this river. That little tin BBQ nailed to a tree stands out like a neon sign for boaters. This is the only place available.

As if on cue, two rafts with a dozen people on board rounded the bend and edged up to the bank. The boaters beat it up the path to the shack, lining up at the bathroom door on their way. Paul hustled to his place in the window. While he was taking care of this group 2 pick-up trucks appeared and 4 more people joined the line.

Paul had them all served in minutes. Their money was registered and the tip jar was anointed. Paul gave every one of his customers a smile and a benediction, "Thanks. Enjoy your Meal."

Paula and Jerry seemed impressed. Paul told them, "Saturday and Sunday will be busy."

Paul quickly prepared take-out barbecue for four people, hung a paper sign that said closed until 2 PM. He figured that he wouldn't be missing too much and that he could clean up later. We might even stay open until dark to make up for the missed hours. He treated the business as if it was his own.

Paul set the lunch out on real plates, with Megan's stainless steel flatware and glasses. He thought it looked nice as they sat to eat together. The river view was pretty and the picnic table and benches gave them ample space.

Presently Paula sat back and said, "That's very, very good. What do you think Jerry? Would you be happy to serve food like this?"

"Sure. I like it fine. Good job Paul. Thanks for feeding us."

Paul gave them all a tour of the trailer and a little lecture about its features. "I find it very comfortable. This is how people hereabouts live. Manufactured housing is the best cost per square foot living space available." He felt like an expert since he had read through Megan's files containing the original mobile home brochures.

As the company was getting into their car Johnny held back a little and said, "I think it's a sale. He's been here before and I had Regan fax all the numbers to Paula last week. I didn't tell you because I wanted to give you peaceful possession as long as practical. Okay?"

"Sure Johnny. If I'd known you were coming I would have spent days cleaning everything up. Thanks."

"Paul. Everything looked fine. You are a good housekeeper."

They sat in the judge's conference table again with two new players: Paula the broker and Jerry Marks the buyer. Johnny's secretary was there to notarize the documentation. There were several purposes for the meeting:

- Convey Megan's property and business to Jerry
- Discharge Paul from any further involvement
- Appoint Johnny as executor off Megan's estate
- Receive appropriate cashier's checks from Jerry to pay the broker's commission, to pay off the bank and to pay Megan's estate the balance.

Paul had to write final checks to Johnny and Regan for final fees. Now that Paul was out of the business, Megan's estate would need to pay them.

There was a veritable raft of paperwork. Paul had to give Johnny final sales tax reports and withholding tax submission forms with checks attached. There were dozens of documents.

When the meeting and the signing were over, Jerry had the keys to the business and the trailer.

Jerry received 1 day's training from Paul. It had not gone well in Paul's opinion. Jerry never worked in foodservice before but he exuded an attitude that he could do it all better. The customers were hicks and jerks and Paul was a dumb kid. He did not like Jerry and Jerry seemed to like no one. And the food was "…for shit."

Paul's worldly possessions were packed in his truck. He was homeless and jobless but somehow satisfied that he had brought a sad situation to a satisfactory conclusion. For once in his life he had done the right thing.

WEDNESDAY, OCTOBER 1, 1997

Paul and Marvin were sitting on a bench in the early October sunlight waiting for Susan and their son Mars.

COC customers, mostly rafters, and employees milled about in the near distance. The day was a gift from heaven. Blue skies and mild temperatures ruled. The slight breeze was pleasant.

“Marvin. It‘s a little early for me to go back to Huntsville. Now that the Shack is gone I’d like to stay here a while to go back to playing on the river.”

So what do you need, a place to stay or a job?”

“Yeah. Both Marv. Who do I talk to?”

“See that woman. Right there.” He pointed, “That’s Betsy, our Personnel Director. Wait here a minute.” Marvin jumped up and approached a woman hanging out with a small group of paddlers. Paul could see that she was young, in her early twenties, and dressed outlandishly in figure-hugging wetsuit and a pink trimmed, tutu-like, spray skirt. She had a pink helmet on her head and matching pink water boots.

Paul saw Marvin gesturing, grinning and pointing at him. After a moment the two left the group and came to Paul. He stood to greet her with a handshake. "Hi. I'm Hunter. Paul Hunter." He was aping the James bond character in the movies. She got it and they smiled at each other.

"Bowman. Betsy Bowman. Pleased to meet you.

"Marv tells me you need a job, a place to stay, and that you'll do anything and work for peanuts. Could this be true?" she asked with an incredulous smile and a shrug of her shoulders.

Paul started to reply but she interrupted him… "He also says that you're his hero and that you are the best man he knows and that is a really good reference."

"Well. Marvin and I are friends. Susan too. I sure will work for peanuts. Do you have anything at this late date?"

"The only thing we really need is a dishwasher at Corney's Cavern Restaurant. Do you know the place?"

"Sure. But I'll need a little training. I haven't worked at a real restaurant. Oh yeah. I forgot. I do have a current Clancy County Health Department Certificate."

"You're hired. The pay is minimum wage and the possibility of tip sharing with wait staff. Marvin will train you if you can start Saturday morning. Most employees pay for the Meal Plan. It gives you three square a day and we deduct the cost from your paycheck.

"What do you say?"

Paul eagerly said yes." And shook her hand. "Thanks. That's great! Is there any paperwork?"

"We'll do the paperwork later - I've got to get on the river now or turn into a zombie. You can stay at the main staff house down the road. It's really just a bunkhouse and shared bathroom. Marvin will show you."

Paul liked bunking with other people for a change. Sharing space and the toilet facilities were not a problem. He was, in fact, far more comfortable than in his tent. He felt more secure too. He'd never had a problem but it was just a thin piece of fabric between him and nature. The COC bunkhouse was not a properly winterized dwelling, but it was a step up from canvas. Living in Megan's trailer had been a mixed blessing because of his emotional state.

Friday night - Paul was never much of a drinker. A little beer. Mostly just a bottle or two. So the staff party should have been a mild night for him. But he had a few more than usual because he was excited about having a real job, because his mates were urging him on, and because he was feeling liberated. He got drunk.

It was a major effort to make it to Corney's Cavern Restaurant at 5 AM. The alarm rang for a long time before he could rouse himself. He felt horrible. He was nauseated, his head was splitting and he was muttering under his breath.

The dishwashing station was a royal mess of greasy pots and pans and stacks of dirty dishes left over from the previous night. The Thursday night fill-in dishwasher had not done a proper job. The stainless steel machine was littered with nasty looking food and grease. It smelled bad and looked disgusting to Paul.

Marvin was waiting. "What's up Bud? You don't look so good.

"S'okay Marvin. I think I have a hangover. I didn't get to bed until after three."

Marvin said sympathetically, "We have an aspirin bottle here. Maybe you could take some with a little OJ."

Paul looked at Marvin with gratitude in his bleary eyes. He could not speak. He turned away from Marvin and vomited on the stack of dirty dishes in machine's main sink.

"Oops. Sorry about that." He rinsed his hands and face in the employee hand sink.

Marvin suppressed a laugh.

"Marv. Thanks but I don't think I could hold anything down right now." He gasped. "Maybe in a little while. I'll be okay. Just show me how this thing works." He was not smiling.

Marvin showed him how to turn the works on and told him that he had to wait for the rinse-water temperature to reach 180° before running the first load. Aside from its messy state, it was an impressive setup. The dishwashing machine was a Hobart. "This is the Cadillac of dishwashers Paul. Learn this and you'll always have a job at any restaurant in the country. Guaranteed!" he laughed trying to cheer Paul up.

Marvin explained the machine and procedures. It was a U shaped table, with a 12-foot long base. There was a 6-foot dirty side where bussers and wait staff could unload dirty dishes on the left. On the right was 6-foot clean side where washed dishes emerged for drying. The washing compartment was centered. The clean dishes came out hot so they dried quickly.

Large racks held 20 dirty plates on their edges, separated from each other, so that the operator could use a conveniently dangling hose to rinse debris into a large sink, before the wash began.

The main sink drain was protected from clogging by a fitted square stainless basket with perforations to let the rinse water flow into the drain, but not the solids.

The basket of rinsed dishes would slide into the washing compartment. The doors, front and rear, opened and closed with a single lever. A rack of clean dishes would roll out to the clean side when the dirty dishes were pushed in. Detergent and rinse agent were fed from easy to replenish bottles. Glasses and silverware had special racks. The powerful wash, rinse cycle took less than a minute.

Paul was impressed despite his queasiness and pain. Marvin showed him the special racks for glasses, cups and flatware. Flatware went through twice – first lying in a jumble on a rack and, second time, vertical in special containers, handles down, to prevent water spots from forming on the business end.

Once a rack of dishes was clean it could be placed on a wheeled dolly. Dollies would support as many racks as one cared to place on them. Usually 4 racks would be high enough. Clean dishes were rolled to the line-cooks or staff cafeteria line. Glasses and silverware would go to the servers' work area.

It was a strong washing system but large pots and pans would need scraping, scrubbing, and hand washing before going through the machine. Paul saw that he had to sanitize the 'clean' side before he could start. He replenished an almost empty rinse agent bottle and then used a wall-mounted hot water hose to wash down the clean side and its tile walls and floor. He used a hand squeegee to get the water off the walls and stainless steel elements of the unit itself. He thought that it looked nice when he finished.

He noticed that he was soaking wet from the waist down but, in his concentration on the task, he forgot how bad he felt and actually began to feel better. Marvin and the other breakfast cooks cheered him on. Peter the shift manager appeared and kindly suggested that Paul don a rubber apron and handed him a pair of rubber gloves.

The servers started at 6 AM and he saw that despite the banter throughout the establishment, everyone worked hard. They were expecting to serve about 200 morning meals including 40 staff in the staff dining room, 120 clinic students taking weeklong whitewater courses, and an unknown number of regular customers. The 120 clinic students would eat box lunches away from COC. There was a special table set up for preparing these lunches

Paul dumped the strainer into a heavy-duty garbage can fitted with a plastic bag. The can was very heavy and mounted on a wheeled dolly. So he rolled it through the kitchen to the dumpster container located by the back door. He was afraid that if the bag got any heavier he wouldn't be able to boost it into the container. The outside air was crisp and soothing.

He began to clean and organize the 'dirty' side. He racked and rinsed plates, glasses and cups first.

When the big gauge on the dishwasher reached the required temperature, he ran 4 racks through the washer and began scrubbing pots.

He soon worked up a sweat and, began to feel in control. He liked the work. The results of his efforts were immediately apparent. Every steaming, squeaky-clean rack was a little success and he soon felt normal. He loved this work. It cured him!

Breakfast was over at 10:30 AM. The time passed quickly. Paul was told that no lunch would be served at this time of year. People, including employees could eat at The Take Out Restaurant. The dinner crew would not start until after noon. Marvin and one other cook continued to work cleaning the kitchen. One server, a paddling friend that Paul knew from the river, vacuumed the dining room. Everyone remained busy even though the restaurant was closed. Paul was learning that food service folks worked hard before and after the public came in and after they left.

Peter sauntered over at noon and said, "Paul. Let me help you wrap this up. I'd like to take you on a tour of COC and then treat you to lunch at the Take Out."

"Great. I'm getting hungry."

Corney's Cavern was the largest building at COC. The first floor was divided into several areas. He knew the kitchen and the general layout but he enjoyed the tour. "The building is only 2 years old. COC staff did most of the construction labor over the 1997-98 winter. It was built the old fashioned way using post and beam construction." Peter was proudly pointing out hand-hewn timbers and the beautiful craftsmanship of the building. "I'm not a carpenter but I learned a lot. My ambition is to build my own home one day using the skills I picked up that winter."

There was a long dining porch looking out over gardens that supplied the restaurant. It looked over the cave entrance that gave the center its name. "They say that it was dug by hand to mine clay by Indians. Really old."

Paul appreciated the attention that he was being given. They went through the staff dining room and up a stairwell with hand hewn stair treads. They walked into the largest room in the building; a room carpeted and high ceilinged that could be used in a variety of ways. For banquets it would sit over a hundred guests. During the season it might be used for overflow dining. There were generous windows looking out over the mountains.

They went through a couple of doorways checking out a storage area, a small laundry room used for napkins and tablecloths, and into the 2-desk restaurant office where he was introduced to Cornelia Johnson.

"Call me Corney," she said by way of an introduction. Glad you could help us out today'" she said as she shook Paul's hand. "Our staff is very seasonal and lots of folks have left for school and winter jobs already. Are you planning to apply for a job here next season?"

"Yes ma'am. I live in Huntsville but, if I work out, I'd like to come back in the spring." He gave her his best smile. "Thanks for having me now."

Peter contributed in a humorous vein, "Corney. He's doing great. He may look funny but he be strong and smart." They all laughed at this jibe.

They walked away and Peter continued his narration, "Corney is a founder of COC. She and her husband Rolf Johnson started small about 25 years ago and built it into this. We are an employee-owned company now. You are a full-time employee now. If you sign up for the 401 plan you'll acquire shares in the company."

The tour continued through the garden, past the cavern entrance, really just a big hole in the hillside now, and to a farmhouse that was now the administrative office.

There he met the company president and filled out a couple of forms for the payroll clerk. He was now legal for the meal plan and staff housing. His employee code was Hunpa. Peter Jackman was Jacpe and Corney was Johco.

The staff lunch was a hamburger and fries. He could have opted for a veggie burger. Paul was able to eat. His hangover was replaced by fatigue and his hands were sore from handling hot dishes and pots. After saying goodbye to Peter he took a nap in his pickup truck. He was free until 5 AM Sunday morning.

He made it back to the employee dining room by closing. He sat with several other employees at a picnic style table. He enjoyed becoming part of a group. He went into the kitchen, which was open to the staff room, and was surprised to see Vila Thompson, the president of the company, washing dishes, wearing his apron. He approached and reminded her that they'd met just before lunch and that he was the morning dishwasher. She was a very short woman with a very big smile. She kept on working, in the job groove, but gave him a greeting and an invitation to chat. She nodded, "How was your first day Paul?'

"Really good. I hope that I left the station in good shape for you."

"No complaints at all. I can't really talk now but I'm glad you said hello. If I stop the mess will overwhelm me." She added, "I like to try my hand at all of the jobs at the center so I can better understand the challenges the staff faces every day. This is a really hard job," she grinned up at him as she rubbed perspiration off her brow with her sleeve. As he turned to leave she bent to her task and he noticed that she was standing on an overturned plate rack.

He left feeling good about his first day. Getting this job had been an adult decision - he was planning for next year. He felt that he would have played this entire year away had it not been for Megan's accident. That would not have been a bad thing but he was feeling mortal and in need of shaping his life. So far COC had treated him very well indeed. The pay wasn't much but the deal included housing, food and good companions. He was careful not to mention his role at the Barbecue Shack and had asked Marvin and Susan to do the same. By spring, he thought, his face would no longer be associated with anything but the river and the dishwashing station.

The weather was benign in the last weeks of the 1997 season. Clear skies, mild sunny days, chill nights, and the smell of wood smoke in the evening air, became his permanent personal signals of fall in the Georgia Mountains. He worked a four-day schedule - some mornings and some nights. Off days were for paddling or hiking amidst the fall colors. The responsibilities that the Shack had imposed were left in his wake. At night he dreamed about Megan. Mostly work scenarios where he had to do things for her. The making slaw ream was his favorite. They had food fights that he let her win.

Paul stopped at the Barbecue Shack on the last Wednesday in October. Jerry sold him a drink and a barbecue pork sandwich. He was not very talkative but he did say, "I'm closing for the season Monday. I'm tearing this crap building down and I'm working on a design to replace it that will be much easier to work. It's gonna be better than paying for a new roof and termite repair bills I'm facing."

“Good luck with that,” Paul replied. “I’m heading home myself and Sunday will be my last day at work.”

“Oh yeah. Where are you working?”

“COC.” Paul wished that he hadn’t told Jerry anything. He didn’t know why but he felt that Jerry was a troubled man and he didn’t want anything to do with him. He swallowed his last bite and carried his drink to the car. “See ya.” He said but Jerry had already turned his back and didn’t seem to care.

Paul was heading for the put-in to meet Marvin for their last paddle of the season. COC’s Guest Appreciation Festival was going on all weekend and he planned to sell his boat and gear at the annual whitewater yard sale.

His money situation was strong. There was more than enough cash in his waterproof wallet to last the year. His COC paychecks and most of the balance in his checking would go to his mother for investing. He didn’t know why he was saving money but he had little urge to spend.

Paul had appointments with both Johnny and Regan for Monday and a plan to stay with Mitch and Molly for a few days in Asheville before heading home to work for his dad and spend the holidays at home.

Paul and Johnny were now close enough to share a bro-hug rather than just a handshake. They met at Johnny’s home and sat on the front porch overlooking a broad lawn and stately trees. His house was right on Route 72 just a mile or so shy of the city line. Few cars passed. They were out of the wind and the sun kept them warm. Paul commented on the ‘For Sale’ sign on the lawn. Madelyn, Johnny’s wife came to sit with them bringing a coffee pot and cookies. The screen door made a little double-bang behind her as she settled down to sit with them.

"Paul. I'm afraid I won't be around much longer and this place is too big for Maddy."

Paul said, "Johnny - are you sick? I'm so sorry."

"I've been sick with kind of blood cancer for a long time. It's a form of leukemia. I don't want to burden you with the details but the docs give me less than a year so we're going to move to Jacksonville, Florida to be closer to our children and grandchildren and leave dear Clancy behind forever.

"But Paul. Remember, I've been around for a long time now. I'm ready for the next world. Try to look on this as a good and natural event. Don't be troubled."

Madelyn said, "Paul. We're both okay with this. I've been wanting to move to Florida for a long time but Johnny's work wouldn't let us. You are his last client." She smiled as she spoke and Johnny seemed so serene that Paul tried to join them in their attitude toward their life cycle.

"They, the docs, have plans for me. I've been to the Mayo in Jacksonville. They suggest that we move quickly, before they start the radiation and stronger meds. Then I might be a candidate for a bone marrow transplant.

"At my age I probably won't be cured but they may get me a few more years. And we don't know how well I'll tolerate the treatment. It could be worse than the disease. I've been feeling a little sick for a long time now." He smiled warmly as he spoke to Paul. He seemed at peace.

They moved the conversation to Paul's plans. "I got a job with COC for next year, I hoped that you'd be around so we could visit once in a while."

"Good for you. What will you be doing?"

"It may not sound like much for educated people like you but I'm going to be a dishwasher at Corney's Cavern Restaurant. You know, the new one on the hill. And I'll be on the reserve Raft Guide Squad on days' off. It's my first real job where I won't be working for my dad. The kindly slave-master." He laughed. "So far I'm really enjoying the work. I like cleaning things up and serving people. Maybe there's a career up there for me. It's an employee owned company with health benefits and a 401K plan."

"Paul. We're not all cut out to be college graduates. The world is made up of two kinds of people: those who are happy with what they do, and those who wouldn't be happy no matter what. They'd complain if you fried them in real butter."

They all laughed at the joke.

"I agree with Johnny, Paul," Madelyn ventured. "Follow your heart and you will find happiness, wealth and satisfaction with the world. Look at me. I graduated from Hofstra University, summa cum laud, with a degree in math science. I worked for years before I met Johnny and I wasn't happy for a day. Now I've been a housewife and mother for over 40 years and I'm as happy as I can be. I love doing the dishes too."

"On another subject Paul. We are closing the book on Megan. We have tried very hard but there are just no clues. We've looked at her papers, her phone and bank accounts, her loan applications, her tax returns and we're at a dead end. There's quite a bit of cash in her estate now that everything's been sold. There was mortgage insurance too. But there is a big hospital bill to be settled by her new representative. I trust him to do the right job. The money will escheat to the State of Georgia eventually. But I have turned everything over to lawyer Bunny Johns. You have a special interest and status as Megan's late guardian. You can go to her if ever you want to find out more."

When the visit was over, Paul said "Johnny. You have my number in Alabama. Call me if you need help with anything. I'll come right away." Paul, emotions easily roused, had tears forming as he waved goodbye to his friends.

After stopping by to see Regan at his accounting office. Paul drove off through the mountains at a measured pace to visit Mitch and Molly in Asheville.

NOVEMBER 1997

The weather in Huntsville was milder than at COC. Paul took one day off and then went to work with his dad on a major home remodeling project. He worked as a laborer to start. He was part of a crew that had been with his dad for years. They were used to bossing Paul around and he did not mind. They sometimes called him 'Twinkle Toes,' remembering an incident when he was in high school. He had kicked over a pan of paint. There hadn't been any real damage but he still wore the work boots he'd had on that day. The right one had a lick of red paint on the right toe.

He was actually a neat and careful worker. He had experience as a rough carpenter, painter, sheet rock hanger and all-around construction skills.

The main job Paul worked on was a remodel involving gutting the kitchen, dining and living areas and tearing down walls to create a sizable great room. His dad was there for a few minutes every morning to check progress, manage supplies and confer with the owners who were living in the basement where they could escape some of the dust and noise.

Demolition was almost done when Paul arrived and by his second week he was laying floors, hanging sheet rock, and fitting floor and crown molding. The hard physical work felt good to Paul. All in all the work was not harder than the restaurant work he had been doing.

His mom and dad were very happy to have him at home and they pumped him for all the details regarding his adventures at the Shack, at COC and on the rivers.

"Did you mind camping out so long," his mom asked at dinner.

"Yes and no. At first it was like vacationing. Like last year. But the weather wasn't always nice and when it turned cold or wet, I longed for my bed at home. When I took over for Megan and lived in her trailer, it felt insanely comfortable. And when they gave me a place in COC staff housing I liked that a lot better than camping too.

"Next year I want to go back to COC."

His parents watched him with wary eyes. They had been talking, with and without Paul, about the possibility of him staying in Huntsville and studying to become a licensed contractor. "What else would you like to do Paul?" they asked.

"I'm embarrassed to say that, long-term, I don't really know. I have an ambition to become a better kayak paddler and maybe a full-time river guide at COC. That thing with Megan turned the year bad for me. I worked and worried myself to death.

"But then they hired me as a dishwasher. I know it doesn't sound like much - I really liked it.

"Dad. This is the first real job I've gotten by myself and I can't wait to get back to it. I love working for you too. Don't get me wrong. I'm not in rebellion. It's just that I feel like working there in the mountains is good for me."

"Right now," his dad pointed out, "we would be able to support you if you want to go to school. So now is good, eh?

"Five or ten years from now we may need you and Mitch to support us." Times are good now but it may not always be so easy for us."

Paul had a healthy bank account. He had worked as Megan's replacement for four months. Carefully following the rules established by the court, he had taken out over $10,000.00. He had given most of it to his mother to add to his investment. He accumulated the tip money in his shirt pocket and had more than $1,000.00 tucked in his pocket now. He was proud of his financial results but he would rather be poor and still have Megan alive and well.

"So Dad. If you'll have me I'd like to work until the first of March. I'm scheduled to report to work on April 4th and I want to take a 3-day whitewater rescue course they offer before I start."

""I only wish you could stay longer. Of course I'll have you."

"Me too," said Mom. Please stay as long as you can and come back home as soon as you can."

MARCH 1, 1998

Paul learned more about the construction business than he anticipated. His dad suffered a health reversal on the second day of March. Paul was unable to return to COC as planned.

It may have started with the fall or, perhaps, with the heart attack. Either way, the result was a broken arm, a broken leg, and a heart attack. He was climbing a ladder with a heavy tool belt on a construction site when it happened. The arm and the leg injuries were obvious; the heart attack was more insidious. The result was a week in the hospital and then confinement to the house until his leg healed enough to get around on crutches. The Hunter's health insurance was limited and did not completely cover the large bills that came flooding in.

There wasn't much damage to his heart. He was placed on a drug regimen to lower his cholesterol and control his blood pressure. He was told that he could look forward to regular medical checkups for life.

Mom and Dad were strong people and could have no doubt been able to survive the problems incurred when it became impossible for him to immediately go back to work. But Paul felt that he had to step up and do the things his parents needed.

"Honey. I know you want to go back to Georgia but it would be a blessing if you could stay until Dad gets back on his feet. We have insurance and savings but frankly we're in trouble.

"As you know a lot of the profit from the work Dad does comes in at the end of the job and not the beginning. He's got 4 jobs underway and there's a 'holdback' in each one of them that doesn't get paid until the final walk-through and punch-list are completed.

"There's about $50,000 in profit to be made from the jobs underway but, if they're not finished properly, there may be no profit at all," his mom was frankly crying. "Paul. I know that this was not a part of your plan. We're asking you first because Mitch and Molly are so involved in Asheville and, frankly, you are more flexible and closer at hand too."

He sat next to her and hugged her, as she had comforted him so many times over the years.

"Mom. I'll do whatever I can. You know that I have no plans for my investment account and I also have $2,000.00 in the bank besides that. I have some cash too. It's all yours. What else do you need?"

"Honey. Thank you, thank you, thank you… It's not so much the money right now. We have to organize things while your dad is laid up and you may be the only one who can do it.

"Between you and me we can keep things going but you must be out on the job for him every day. Be his eyes and ears and keep in close touch with his customers and employees."

There were several jobs underway at the moment. A $20,000-basement apartment, the $25,000-kitchen remodeling, a $150,000-home addition, and a $50,000-sunroom, garage combination. The basement apartment was almost finished and the others nowhere near completion. The promise dates were clear and Paul could see that he would not be a dishwasher-paddler-raft guide and free spirit this year.

Paul reviewed the paperwork with his mother and father. Contracts, material receipts, bills, time sheets, and such, in manila folders. There was one jacket for each project. There was a ledger sheet stapled to each folder to allocate expenses. Some jobs were more profitable than others. The larger the contract the greater the risk of miscalculation and misfortunes. There was a hand-wrought calendar on the front of each folder to help schedule the many jobs required to produce a finished project.

His dad was a good record keeper but the primary force behind each job was not in the record keeping. It was in the relationships with customers, workers, suppliers, subcontractors, inspectors, permit authorities, unions, competitors, utility companies and the banks.

There were 7 employees including Paul – each one he thought more experienced than himself. He was not full of confidence, and he was afraid that he would make mistakes. When he confessed his doubts to his father he expected comforting words.

"Paulie. Don't worry about how you feel. Just make sure the other guy sees that you are interested in him, his point of view and his welfare. If you act confident and happy, that's how people will see you. It's an act for all of us.

"If you don't have the answer to a question or a problem, have the balls to admit it. Remember these words. 'Let me get right back to you on that.'

"Nobody much cares about how you feel or what you like, other than your family and friends. They care about their stuff but they will like you, help you and trust you if you care about their stuff too.

"What do you think about that?" His dad was sitting in his armchair with his legs elevated.

"Let me get right back to you on that." They both laughed.

Paul crafted a plan with his dad. He started by carefully prioritizing his time. He had a talk with each owner assuring them that their work would be done properly and on time. He told the employees that their jobs and paychecks were secure.

He told each employee and supplier, "You know, this may be a good thing. There is a great crew of workers and fine subs to do the work. Now Dad can concentrate on selling and estimating new jobs. He's the brains. I'm just his feet and eyes."

Paul did a lot of chores around the house too. He mowed the lawn, kept the gardens neat and took care of garbage can and other mundane tasks usually done by his dad. He shaved every morning and visited the barber every second Saturday.

He was quite over Sarah. She had not given him the slightest encouragement on the few school breaks when he had called her at home. Her words reverberated in his head, "I do like you Paul but I'm hell bent on getting my degree, my doctor and a rich life in the suburbs. I think you should get over it and not call again. I mean this as a kindness honey. I don't want to string you on or to get derailed myself."

They both cried as they rang off. Paul was fully convinced and ready to move on to other women.

March 17, 1998

Friday was payday and the crew usually met at Duffy's Tavern for the beer and chicken wing specials after work. These men he worked with were mostly married and he usually found himself alone before the clock rang seven. His folks had approved the idea of his picking up the tab as a company expense. Paul had to limit himself to coke since he was not yet twenty-one.

The Tavern hired extra help on Saint Patrick's Day. He met a temporary server named Irene Linnick there on that special Tuesday holiday and she had caught his eye with her unusual grace and strength as she managed heavy trays, pitchers of beer and baskets of wings. She had red hair and an animated face with frequent outbursts of humor and jokes. She kidded Paul as his tablemates left him alone at the regular hour. "You forgot your deodorant honey?" she joked as she cleared the table.

"Nah. I just can't find the right kind of friend," he replied. "I need someone who has more endurance. Are you available?"

""Not tonight honey. I'm heading for the barn as soon as they let me off. I have to get up at seven o'clock in the morning."

"Me too," said Paul. "I'm in construction. What are you taking? He had her pegged as a student.

"I'm studying for my AA in Outdoor Recreation at UAH. I'm thinking resort management. I teach dancing. Ballet and jazz in the evenings. Gotta go." She bounced off but when he paid the tab for himself and his crew he got her phone number and gave her his business card.

Paul Hunter
Hunter and Company
Construction Management

Paul was proud of his card. He was not yet 20-years old but felt like an old hand now with heavy coaching from his parents and OJT.

Irene sounded very reserved when he called her the next evening. Reserved and tired.

"Irene. Would you like to go out with me this weekend? Say a movie and dinner?"

"I'm a little overscheduled right now Paul. I don't really date but I eat every day. Would you like to have dinner with me?

"I'm busy too. I don't really date either, but I sleep every night. Would you like to sleep with me one evening soon?" There was a shocked silence on the line. Then Irene burst out laughing… At first a titter, then a guffaw… "Paul. You are a darling. Let's have dinner first."

They both laughed and finally settled down. "Irene. You know I'm just kidding. I'm really not this bold. You are literally the first girl I've ever called for a date. I don't date either.

"I'm not overbooked and I can make it any night but Sunday. I always have family dinner with my mom and dad on Sundays. Sometimes my brother drives all the way from Asheville to be there with his girlfriend. I can make it any night you choose. What's best for you? Your call entirely. Time, place and day. You could even meet my folks."

"I'm sure I'll love your folks but let's get to know each other first. Okay?"

"Sure."

"Friday night I don't have classes. I usually crash and burn, but I could rise to the occasion if Friday is good for you."

"Perfect. I can pick you up any time or if you'd like to come to Duffy's we can go from there. Or I could pick you up anywhere. I usually hang out there for a little while on Fridays. I get there at around five with the guys from work."

"Good there's fine. I'll meet you at Duffy's at six. Can we go to Argos on the river? Dutch."

"No. No. I'll pay. This is my…"

"Dutch. Double Dutch," she said. "That way I can order anything I want. Or I could pay for you but you'll have a limit of…"

"No limits. No limits. We can go Dutch this time but I really want to treat you next time. When we get to know each other a little.

"But look. There's something else. I'm coming directly from work. Please can I just wear my jeans and I'll put on a sports coat for dinner. Very California ya know. Would that be okay?"

"Sure. Me too. I'll dress California."

The spring weather was sublime, and work was good. He was feeling very relaxed and in a playful mood when he met Irene at the bar. He'd had his usual coke but offered Irene a drink before going to dinner.

She declined saying, "Paul. I don't drink and I don't date." She looked at him with a friendly smile when she said this. Her California consisted of designer jeans, a fuzzy red sweater and red shoes with 2-inch heels.

She seemed to glow. Paul guessed it was the reflected color from the sweater but she looked hot in his eyes. "You go ahead and have another. I don't mind."

Paul wore a white turtleneck shirt with jeans and a tweedy jacket. Irene thought he looked fine. He seemed to have plenty of energy and she liked the way he moved. He had real muscle under his clothing.

"I have to admit that I don't drink either. I had a few too many one night last fall to celebrate getting a job at the Caverns Outdoor Center in Georgia. It made me sick on my first day at work. I vowed to quit."

"COC. You gotta be kidding! I go to school with people who work there in the summer." She gave him several names but he didn't know them."

"There are a lot of people there. I came in just 4 weeks before the end of the season."

"I'm supposed to be working there now." He went on to explain his dad's injuries and illness.

They left Duffy's tavern in Paul's pickup truck. He was on his best behavior. He held the restaurant door for her and opened the truck door too. He made sure she was well seated before he closed the door. Irene smiled her appreciation for the formalities. The truck was more battered than ever but the inside and the glass were spotless. He wanted to make a good impression on Irene.

They were seated in a booth at Argos. They ordered steaks and cokes. Their sides were identical and they both said medium when the waiter asked them how to cook the meat.

They grinned at each other across the table. Paul offered her a high five and a grin. She reciprocated saying, "Fine choices!"

They enjoyed the intimacy of sharing a meal in a nice restaurant. Candlelight, white tablecloths, and expert service moved things along and they lost track of time.

"Too bad about your dad," she commiserated. "How is it going?"

"Dad's doing well. His heart attack was minor. A warning the doctor said to take better care of his health." He launched into telling her about the jobs they had working and the relief he had felt when he finished the punch list on the basement apartment and the joy at getting the check for the balance. "That check represented the entire profit for the job. The prepayments and progress payments had gone entirely towards materials and labor. So my folks are solvent at the moment.

“Dad thinks he has sold another job to begin in July. He’ll be on crutches but he ought to be able to get out and about on a limited basis. Now it’s just back and forth to the doctors’ offices. I’m taking care of supervising the jobs, under his supervision. Plus I do carpentry, sheet rock and painting. Not so much electrical or plumbing.”

“Wow Paul. You must know a lot about the construction business. Do you want to continue that line of work when your dad’s better?”

“No,” he said slowly. “I think I want to go back to working at COC and being a river rat. Just messing about in kayaks.” He told her about working at the Barbecue Shack and camping out but did not tell her about the real events and Molly’s demise. He felt that those details about his life were still too raw for casual conversation.

“I wish I had a career goal but it just hasn’t hit me yet. What do you want to do Irene? Like, I mean besides your school?”

“Well. I’m not too driven either. I worked some in restaurants in the summers and after school. It’s kind of addicting. I can see why you liked it at COC.

“My mom took me to dance classes when I was little. I studied ballet and jazz. When I got to my teen years I was so into it that I began to work, without pay, as a teacher’s assistant with the little beginners. I just sort of grew into a paid employee. When I began college it was paying me enough to get an apartment with schoolmates. My folks still pay my school expenses. I’m 21 so that won’t last much longer. Dad’s an architect and Mom is a domestic goddess.”

“Oops. You’re an older woman,” Paul grinned. I’ll be 20 this year.”

"Sigh," she breathed. "You're too green kid. I guess I'll have to put you back for a while."

"Oh please. Just let me sit in the sun for a little bit and I'll be all right."

They passed on dessert. When the check came they left a 20% tip and thanked the waiter profusely. He had just let them sit without feeling neglected. He was glad that he didn't have to ID them.

Paul held doors and when they got back to her car at Duffy's, he politely escorted her to the door. "Irene," he asked her through her car window, "Would you like to do this again?"

"Sure. Could we wait for Friday though? This is really my best night."

"Sure. Oh, and can I follow you home to see you safe."

"Nope. I'm fine. It's been a long day for both of us. Call me. Okay?"

"Good. Will do. Drive safe."

He stepped back as she started the car and they smiled goodnight. He admired her posture and felt that he had missed an opportunity to shake hands or give her a kiss on the cheek. No matter, he thought. I had a great time.

JULY 1998

The weeks slipped by and Mike Hunter recovered his abilities. The casts came off and he walked - at first with a cane, then with a limp. The limp would go away by the end of the month as exercise and activity restored his muscle function to previous levels. He had lost a few pounds but was ready to work as a construction supervisor, perform as a salesman of home remodeling projects and recover his place as man of the house.

Mike's work was easier now with Paul as his alter ego. Paul had saved the Hunter fortunes and both he and Sam, as he was wont to call his wife, made sure that Paul knew their gratitude. "Paul," his dad said at Saturday dinner, "You've done a great job. Everyone I've talked to has nothing but praise for 'Young Hunter.' Thanks for being you."

With his dad getting back in the saddle, Paul's work was easier too. They had 2 new projects and Paul participated in the planning and preliminaries. He saw that his dad approached authorities in the building department permit sections with a humble and respectful attitude. He learned, from him, to establish better relationships with competitors and suppliers.

He and Irene had continued Friday dinners. She was becoming Paul's unattainable dream girl. He wanted to progress to a deeper, sexual relationship, but she was not having any.

"Paul. I have to confess something," she said anxiously.

"Don't worry Irene. What is it?" They were at their regular table at the Argo Restaurant. Dinner was done and they were speaking very quietly.

After a long pause, Irene ventured, "Paul. I know that you want to have sex with me. And I like you too that way. But I'm damaged goods. What I haven't told you is that I got knocked up in high school, got married to my boyfriend and lost the child to spina bifida. I gave birth but the docs couldn't save her.

"I went into a funk and our marriage was busted." Irene was crying and her head was down as she spoke.

Paul got up to sit next to her and put his arm around her. "I'm so sorry Irene. I see you lost two people you loved at the same time. How long ago was this?"

"Going on 4 years now. I made such a mess. I felt retarded." He hugged her and she turned her head toward him for a salty kiss on the wet cheek."

"I have something to confess too," he told her.

"Wait Paul. You don't have to. I really appreciate your comfort. Thank you. But there is something else I have to tell you. Something you won't like.

"I made a vow when Robby took off. I decided that I wouldn't have sex again until *after* marriage. I love sex and the intimacy it brings, but I just think I owe it to the world, my parents and myself to abstain. I'm now officially saving myself for marriage. Got to put the horse before the buggy this time." She was crying and embarrassed again. He hugged her hard and returned to his seat.

"Gosh I'm sorry about what happened. I can see that it was rough and that you are on a path. You know, I can learn from you.

"I had a bad experience last year that I haven't told anyone but my family in Huntsville." He told her the outline of his affair with Megan and her death.

"You've got me thinking. Men can take a vow of chastity too and it might be the best thing for me too. I feel so guilty about what happened that being, what d'ya call it, celibate, might be a good way for me too.

"Irene. Maybe we could be non-fucking buddies. What do you say?" he meant what he said even though he wanted to jump her right there in the restaurant. He said it as a kind of joke, trying to get her back to an even keel.

She looked at him levelly and said, "Paul. You are a lovely man. That might be too hard for us. Maybe we should switch off the regular Friday thing and let our emotions settle down now that we know the truth about each other."

"Only if you insist. I'm not doing anything on Friday."

He turned off the lights and engine when he parked in front of her apartment. He turned to her and dragged her into a hug. She willingly came in for a kiss too and did not pull back when he stroked her back through the thin fabric of her blouse. He wanted to hold her harder and was drawn to grope her breasts. She sensed his need and moved his hand from her waist to her chest. He felt both the lean hardness of the dancer and the softness of a woman.

"Paul. I want you too but it's so hard right now."

He interrupted her with a chuckle. "Ooh I know what ya mean."

"Please Paul. I don't want to be a tease. If we don't stop now I'm going to wet my panties."

"Me too," he confessed. They both laughed and the spell was weakened. He jumped out and rushed to get her door before she could get out.

They kissed goodnight at the side of the truck. Her lips were soft and moist. Their thighs met and he felt her against his chest. "Good night Irene, good night Irene," he crooned. "I'll see you in my dreams."

She gave him a big smile and walked away lightly, her dancer's body strong against the earth's pull. Paul leaned against the truck and sadly watched her disappear into the apartment building's shadow.

He remembered a joke that Mitch had told him once when they were younger teenagers. They were walking home after school. "Hey Paul. Do you want to meet my girlfriend?"

"Sure," Paul glanced at his brother who grinned and stuck his hand out as if to shake hands. He had a big grin on his face as Paul innocently reached out to shake.

Mitch held the shake a tad longer than expected and burst out laughing. Paul had just shook hands with Mitch's 'Girlfriend.'

He smiled as he drove home for a date with his own girlfriend. Irene's beautiful image danced in his head.

Irene moved to Miami when she graduated in December. They had eased away from their Friday dinners because their sex urge was making them both uncomfortable. But they spoke on the phone every week and, before she left, Irene invited him to attend a dance recital held by her school at the Huntsville Civic Auditorium. "This is a big deal for us Paul. The kids, the teachers and the parents look forward to it each year. It is not a professional grade show, but you'll be surprised at how good the kids are. Especially mine – I mean the little ones. We'll fill the theater for 2 shows."

Paul asked his parents to come but his dad had a conflict. He and his mom arrived at the theater at 6 PM. There was a good crowd but they had prime reserved seats and Paul did enjoy the show. His mom was thrilled that he had asked her. "Will I get to meet the mysterious Irena?"

"Irene." He corrected her. "Sure Mom. Maybe we could take her to dinner."

Samantha was excited to finally meet one of Paul's few girlfriends. She had never met Megan, of course, but she had shaken hands with Sarah at graduation.

The dance teachers had all received bouquets from their students on stage after the performance. So Samantha easily recognized Irene as she approached them on the theater steps afterwards, carrying her flowers. She was struck by her beauty and grace.

They did not have dinner as Irene was heading for her parents' home for a farewell Saturday supper. She and Paul hugged hard. This was their goodbye.

Paul had a tear in his eye as he drove his mom's car home. "I'm really sad to see her go. She got a great job with the Marriott Hotel in Miami. We had a good friendship and I wish it could have gone further Mom. But I'm drawn to return to COC and the Clancy River next spring. I don't want to work in construction right now. I don't know why but I feel compelled to go."

"Honey. Dad and I understand. You have many, many years ahead. You will find the perfect path and we'll always be proud of you." She smiled and put a comforting hand on his leg. "And Dad will always have a job for you.

"Paul. Try to stay in touch with your friends even when they are far away."

MARCH 1999

Paul was back at COC on the fourth Saturday of the month. He was scheduled to start work as a dishwasher on Sunday. He was happy with his assignment to a 3-bedroom cottage with 5 other restaurant employees. He spent the day organizing his bunk area, cleaning his truck, and shaking hands with everyone he met. There were no old faces.

Paul drove past the Barbecue Shack and had a kind of mental pause and confusion he had never experienced. What the hell…? he thought…wasn't that where…?

He pulled over, backed off the road and slowly returned to the shack's parking lot. It wasn't there! The parking area was overgrown with foliage and fallen leaves. There was no trace of the actual building or concrete foundation. Even the utility pole was gone. He got out of his truck and poked around, unable to figure out what catastrophe had occurred here. The path to the river was overgrown and his former campsite looked just like the rest of the forest floor.

He made his way down to the river and sat on a boulder for a few minutes remembering Megan, his peaceful time in a tent by the river, and his sorrowful summer of waiting for his friend to die. He stroked his beard and wiped away a tear. He was set on a course – to fit in at COC. His hair was shaggy but not yet long enough for a ponytail.

He drove the few miles to COC and stopped in at the front desk. He did not recognize the young woman at the desk. She greeted him with a smile, thinking he was an off-season guest.

"Hi. I'm Paul Hunter. I work here but I skipped last season. Do you know what happened to the Barbecue Shack that used to be a couple of miles up-river? I used to work there"

"No. I never saw it last year but I may have heard that the owner was going to demolish it and couldn't get a permit to rebuild.

"Look for one of the old-timers at the store. They'll probably know."

He thanked her and reported for work up the hill.

At dinner, in the small staff cafeteria, he was happy to see shift manager Peter Jackman sitting at an indoor picnic table with several other employees. Peter asked Paul to join the table.

He met the general manager of the restaurant, Archie and a couple of instructors. They all gossiped about winter activities that included world travel as COC whitewater trip leaders to Nepal and South America. Others at the table had worked at ski resorts and one had a Christmas tree business. Paul was very impressed and began to see some benefits of the seasonality of the COC business.

Paul found out that Marvin and Susan had moved to Florida to be with aging parents. They were his only close friends from 1997 - *Megan's Year,* as he liked to call it. He asked Peter if it would be possible to get an address for Marvin and Peter said he'd try.

No one remaining at the center knew of Megan's tragic love affair and her sad ending. Only Paul remembered. It was a sadness that he carried with him. He threw himself into his dishwashing duties and spent days off on the river in his new kayak or waiting for work as a raft guide.

Paul ventured to Clancy a few weeks after his return and looked for Sam Silver, the State's Attorney that he and Johnny had worked with. Sam was cordial and seemed to have plenty of time for them to catch up on each other's lives. They had a friendly visit

"Paul. You know that Johnny passed away?"

"He told me he had very little time just before he moved to Florida. I didn't know that he died. I really liked him."

Sam knew exactly what had happened to the Barbecue Shack.

"Damn shame. There was a huge conflict with that guy Jerry Marks. About 2 years ago. Just after you left. He all of a sudden tore the place down, hauled away the debris and then applied for a permit to build a little better, more modern facility. Not very big.

“But they couldn’t give him a permit. Clancy County had an agreement with the state and the USDA to not permit any new construction on the river for 10 years, to give authorities time to work out a plan to designate the Clancy as a Wild and Scenic River. It’s a valuable program with the Bureau of Land Management National Park Service US Fish and Wildlife Service US Forest Service and the state of Georgia. No one here really knows if it can happen but the County was obligated to deny the building permit.

“Jerry could have updated or improved on the existing footprint if he had applied before a complete demo, but he was impatient and he paid a heavy price.

“He’s gone now. There was no law suit but I think it was close.”

A few weeks later, Paul spent some quiet time at his special, ‘secret garden’ on the river. He thought again about Megan and her fear of the water. He mused about Jerry’s abrupt and rather bad attitude. And about his own failings.

He decided that he was happy with a simple life. Sometimes he took pleasure from being on his own. His problems seemed few.

Paul liked to watch the cooks perform their duties and, without thinking much about it, learned a lot of their routines and duties. There was a particular cook that he enjoyed watching and talking to as she worked. She was Eddie Mitchell, half of a husband and wife team there for the summer. Her husband, Slim, was the baker, producing bread, rolls, pizza, pastries and other items for the clinics and public tables. Eddie was the prep cook responsible for doing prep work for the entire kitchen operation including the restaurant, the staff cafeteria and the clinic dining service.

She was a graduate of the Culinary Institute of America, known as the CIA, had a professional set of cooking skills and was happy to show them off whenever Paul had time to watch or had questions.

Eddie was good with her knives. She did not share her tools with the other cooks who all used house knives and tools. She brought them to work in a special briefcase and sharpened selected knives before clocking in.

She would process whole bags and crates of vegetables at the start of each shift. Cleaning, peeling, slicing, dicing and otherwise getting everything ready to be cooked for the evening meal. After the prep she would cook the evening meal for the clinics and that item would also serve as the staff meal and the daily special in the restaurant. Her movements were economical, her tools sharp and her techniques interesting – different from anything he had seen while growing up in and about his mother's kitchen.

Eddie was not a happy go lucky person. She would mutter things about her fellow cooks, the wait staff, the kitchen layout and her husband Slim. Like "Piss-poor preparation produces piss-poor performance," or "*mise en place, mise in place,*" over and over again.

She would take a few minutes before each shift to make sure that she had the recipes and specs together for each item on her job list along with the actual foodstuff, tools, storage pans, pots and platters. This was the *mise en place* procedure. Her work volume seemed overwhelming to the uninitiated, like Paul, but she flew through each project, never leaving her station until it was time to deliver something or time to assemble a dish for cooking.

Head down, muttering, hands flying, a bag of carrots would suddenly become plastic containers full of sliced carrots. Potatoes would lose their skins, have a bath and be evenly diced or sliced for further cooking operations.

Eddie told Paul that she had been a cook in the army and that her service benefits had paid for her degree in culinary arts. She and Slim had been in the army together. She said he was was a Blue Cord infantry soldier.

Paul had never heard of the CIA and was very impressed by all she said. The buzz in the kitchen was that she was here for only one season and that Corney and Archie expected that everyone would learn from her.

Corney's Cavern Restaurant was widely known for its food quality due to several important factors. The breads they made were freshly crafted every day. The biggest sellers were tender beef shish kebab marinated in honey, oil and teriyaki sauce, and local farm-raised trout. Cornelia Johnson's food had a lot of style and was appreciated by all who sampled it.

The salads served with every dinner were presented with Corney's secret-formula ramp dressing and decorated with an edible flower. The blossoms came from the garden and the ramps from the forest.

Corney would spend days wandering the forest every spring to gather ramps in burlap sacks. The ramps would be cleaned and frozen in quantities sufficient for the entire season. Pungent, finely chopped ramps would be mixed with sour cream, buttermilk and other seasonings every week. No one loved this forest bounty more than Corney. The salads were one of her signatures.

Eddie seemed an odd bird with her checkered pants, black military dress shoes, short stature and attitude. Everyone was in awe of her including her husband Slim. She recognized a desire to learn in Paul's eyes and she would give him mini-lessons in cooking each time he visited her station.

"Paul. You see that I am the only cook in this kitchen who has my own tool kit." She opened the briefcase she carried into the kitchen each day and pointed out some knives and their cost.

He was flabbergasted. "$100.00 for a single knife. Wow. I hope they're paying you big bucks here."

"Naw. We're here for the fun of it. Slim's just learning to bake and I'm his coach. When we go back to real life after the summer we'll worry about getting bigger salaries. These knives are heirloom quality and they'll be around for my children's children." She laughed at the thought of her knives' afterlife.

"This toolkit was a part of the CIA training. I had to buy the stuff at the school bookstore or at a local restaurant supply company. If you want to be a cook I suggest that you visit a restaurant supply company and assemble a kit of knives and a carrier. Could be just a simple canvas roll-up. You'll need a sharpening kit, a sharpening steel and a few knives.

"Buy commercial and they'll be heavy duty but not so expensive. You'll just have to sharpen them more often. To tell you the truth the government paid for these tools along with tuition and books. Slim chose to go to community college and he has an AA in outdoor recreation leadership. That's what pointed us here toward COC. Who knows? Maybe we'll come back every summer from now on."

Paul learned a lot from Eddie and he took his day off with them to go to a large restaurant equipment store in Atlanta's outskirts. They planned dinner and a movie afterwards. Paul made a deal with the couple, "I'll drive and buy lunch and you advise me on how tool up to be a self-trained chef.

"I want to read some books, hang out at your station and practice on COC time. Maybe I can snag a promotion sometime." He had already confessed to her that he had a little cash burning a hole in his pocket and that he'd like some decent tools.

He wound up buying 3 knives, a sharpening steel, a sharpening stone and several little books about sauces, meat cooking methods and restaurant operations. He also bought a canvas roll-up with tie strings to carry the knives to and from work. The cost for the whole lot was just over a hundred dollars.

"Don't worry," Eddie said. "If you start cooking in a big restaurant one day, you can always upgrade to more expensive gear. Chances are though that you will never wear these knives out."

The 10-inch blade chef's knife was the most expensive buy. It was made very strongly. It was very sharp and heavy. He liked the feel of it.

"I'll teach you how to use these guys if you want to come in a little early tomorrow." said Eddie. You too Slim. Sit in on the lesson please."

Slim who had been following them around, admiring the endless parade of stainless steel tables and gadgets, agreed. They set a date for a 10 AM meeting as they drove to see *Primary Colors.*

Eddie's demonstration attracted several other cooks besides Paul. She began by sharpening her chef's knife and laying it out on a large poly cutting board along with a peeler and a folding slicing machine, she called a mandolin. She taped her copies of the day's menu and prep list that had been supplied by the shift supervisor.

She needed to prep a box of romaine lettuce, a box of iceberg lettuce, a bag of potatoes, a bag of onions, a bag of carrots and several other items as well. The items were neatly stacked near her workstation as well as the clean containers and tools that would be needed. She had to cook 125 portions of beef stew to be served to clinic guests, staff and the public as the daily special. She needed to produce a large pot of mashed potatoes, 125 portions, and a vegetarian entrée for 25 as an entrée for the staff vegetarians. She already had a dozen frozen cherry pies in the oven – part of the daily special. "Everything I will use is *mise en place*. On hand and ready to use. She had the spices and other ingredients all at hand.

Eddie began to lecture about knife skills. How to be safe above all else as a cut would slow a cook down or even put him out of action. And it was nasty and painful too.

Peeling carrots first, her peeler flew, working in both directions. The peels landed on the stainless table and in the lined garbage bag she kept at her side. The carrots landed in her prep sink for a wash before further processing into shredded and sliced carrots. She kept her head down and began to hum.

Suddenly, without warning, as the little crowd watched her techniques, she flung her head back and yelled, “Shit! Oh fucking Christ!” She banged the knife onto her board, whirled around and ran to the oven where her pies were giving off smoke. Her nose had tipped her off before the others noticed. She had forgotten to set a timer.

“Damn! I forgot. My fault. Fuck me hard!” Her red face was screwed into a frown as she removed the three large sheet pans holding a dozen smoking pies. The outer edges of the crusts were black.

They expected her to dump them but she fooled everyone by announcing, “Peter. Take the pie off the menu. We’re having cobbler instead.

“Paul. Bring me 12 dozen monkey dishes.” While Paul ran to get the little plates she began knocking the black edges into her garbage can and placed the pies on a clean area of her table. She got a large ice cream scooper and neatly scooped the unburned parts of the cherry pies into the little monkey dishes. She had over a hundred cobblers in a flash.

“Peter,” she commanded, “$3.95 each,” as she placed the dishes onto clean baking sheets and then onto a rolling rack. “No waste. The burned portions go to the gardener with the mulch.

“Slim. Clean these aluminum pie tins up and do something with them.” Her speed was impressive and she finished peeling the carrots before the smoke had been sucked out the kitchen exhaust fans.

Eddie began cutting the carrot ends off into her garbage pans and then slicing them on her 'mandolin'. She had the slices into a pot of water on her stove before she began shredding some for salad garnish.

Her next job was the romaine lettuce. The carrot mess and the pie goof were behind her. The audience dispersed except for Peter and Paul who were not needed for prep. She dipped the lettuce, four heads at a time into a sink full of cold water to knock the dirt off them with the heads down to let the sand and other debris flow into the sink.

She refilled the sink with clean water and dunked the heads several times until her standards for clean lettuce were satisfied. She set the lettuce aside, leafy part down, to enable the water to drain off for a while before further cleaning and processing.

Eddie stopped to hone her knives with the steel sharpener several times during the demo.

The audience left and Eddie really picked up speed. She needed a coffee break and a smoke as soon as possible. Almost all of the cooks used cigarettes and had a regular smoking area well away from the kitchen's back door.

Over the next few weeks she continued to start an hour earlier than scheduled for training and demonstrations. Eddie was rapidly attaining high status as a skilled kitchen worker and other cooks began to emulate her ways when doing prep.

Paul came in early to hang out with Eddie and Slim. He began to know more about cooking and restaurant work as she shared her professional training. She had attended cooking schools while in the army and then had gone to culinary school, full-time, for 2 years and She was a pro with practical ways to handle every kitchen situation, from over-seasoned dishes to substitutions for missing ingredients.

She used her sharp knives to create flowers and little animal statues from a wide variety of ordinary vegetables. "Paul," she confessed, "I didn't make this stuff up. I got it out of books and magazine articles."

Paul was the star dishwasher in the 1999 season. He became an expert paddler, gained experience as a raft guide and learned to cook. He was cooking on the line or prep-cooking several days a week.

Socially he was not so successful. He had work and paddling friends but no matter how hard he tried he could not find a girl to hold. He had his memories and hope for the future. At the Friday night staff party he was always a shy loner and he always abstained from a second bottle of beer.

The college students had to go back to school toward the end of the season and COC was, as usual, short of help. That's how Paul learned to wait on tables.

Peter approached him one busy Saturday night at 8 PM and said, "Paul. We need help in front. Would you please put on a clean server's apron and help us out." A raft guide was washing the dishes and Eddie was working the line with Paul. She was so fast that Paul was not really needed.

"Sure. I don't know much about it but I can learn fast."

His first table was a 4-top. First-timer-tourist types. He was asked a series of questions.

"Do you serve alcohol?

"What's the special of the day?"

"How is the shish kebab made?"

He gave them a big smile and said politely, "Sorry. No booze but you can bring your own if you have it. The beef stroganoff special ran out at 5:30." He knew because he had cooked it.

"Marinated top sirloin with onions, peppers and cherry tomatoes. Cooked to order, served on rice pilaf - it's to die for.

"I recommend the kebabs or the trout.

"Where ya 'all from? What can I bring you to drink?"

His answers to their questions and his own little barrage of questions and obvious good will obviated his need to explain to them that he had never waited on a table before. They were from New York City and wanted water and 4 wine glasses. They all ordered kebabs, medium, and one of them left for their car to get a bottle of wine while Paul disappeared to fetch water and wine glasses.

"Peter. I need a corkscrew and a bucket of ice. Can you help me?"

"Sure Paul. When you're ready, take table 9. Six-top. They'll be seated before you get back."

Paul hustled to get four glasses of water and four empty wine glasses. He had to compete with other servers in the service area for room for his tray, for the glasses, for the ice and even for the water. He was a little surprised that it was so hard to arrange.

Peter had set up the ice bucket and Paul arrived at the same time as the wine. He offered to open it but the guests said no need. "We're starved. Can we be served soon?"

He left the glasses and said, "Absolutely. Right on it!"

He greeted his second table before returning to the kitchen. Big smile. "Sorry the special is out. Have you tried the shish kebab or trout? Can I bring you something to drink while you're deciding?"

They wanted cokes and iced tea.

Paul thought to himself, this ain't too hard but I'd better write something down soon. He paused in the kitchen and wrote his first order and turned it in to the line cooks. He was familiar with the tickets and the timing involved because he worked the line from time to time.

He got a large tray and loaded it with 10 salads, 3 loaves of herb and onion bread, 6 glasses of ice and pitchers of coke and iced tea. The salads had little ceramic containers of ramp dressing. Each loaf of bread sported a little ramekin of butter and a knife. The load was heavy but he was strong and was accustomed to handling the large trays with non-slip, rubberized surfaces from bussing tables and from toting things in the kitchen. He centered his hand, palm up, bent his legs to lift the weight and steadied an edge of the heavy tray on his shoulder. He picked up a folding tray in his other hand as he passed into the dining room. It seemed natural to him and he tried to move deliberately and efficiently rather than hustling like some servers did.

He delivered 4 salads and 2 loaves of bread to his first table and said, "Here's your starter. Your order is in. Can I get anything else now?" They seemed happy so he turned his attention to the other table. His folding tray stand was in place and he gave them the glasses of ice and pitchers of soda.

They ordered 2 trout and 4 shish kebab and were pleased when he immediately began placing the bread and salads in front of them.

Peter intercepted him on his way to the kitchen and said, “Well done. Can you take one more table now?”

“Sure.”

“Table 12. A 4-top.” I’ll seat them now.”

When Paul placed his second order Eddie told him, “Paul. Tone down the shish kebab a little. We’re going to run out if we don’t get more balanced orders.”

“Okay. Sorry.” He grinned and shrugged in apology.

He appeared at his 3rd table with 4 salads, a loaf of bread and four glasses of ice. “Hi folks. No special tonight. Everything else is delish.”

He faintly heard his name and “Order up,” from the kitchen as he took an order for iced tea.

“I’ll be back in a flash for your order,” he told the new table and marched to the kitchen to load up his first dinner order. The kebabs looked and smelled wonderful to him. He placed a steak knife on each platter, added a pitcher of tea to the tray hoisted the load.

The dining room was humming, every table full and a short line waited at the host station. He delivered the tea and kebabs, removing the empty salad plates as he placed the platters in front of each guest. “Paul. Order up,” He heard again, faintly, thru the din.

“What else can I get you?” he asked as he went from diner to diner removing the skewers with a napkin and fork in each hand. They were happy.

Table 3 was eating their salads as he took their order for trout, kebabs and roast chicken. Their salads and bread were under attack. He took their tea pitcher for a refill.

Peter waylaid him as he walked to pick up his next order. "Paul. Can you take a 2-top?"

"I think so."

"Table 11. I'll seat them in a minute."

Paul hurried to the kitchen to pick up his third table's entrees and a pot of tea for refills along with 2 new salads, a loaf of bread and 2 glasses of ice. He delivered the food, took the order from table 4 and saw that table 1 was ready for dessert. They declined dessert and said, "just bring us a check when you can. No hurry. Good job tonight Paul. Your manager told us we were your first table."

"Yep. It was a pleasure. Thanks for being patient. Any suggestions?"

"Yes. Don't change a thing. You're a natural. You made us feel at home."

Table 1 had a check of $67.00 and they left a $20.00 tip. Table two, the 6-top left him $12.00. The evening ran by quickly in a blur of greeting, feeding, checking and pocketing tips. Paul was exhausted by the time the last guest left and cleaning up began in earnest. The servers, mostly local women, were very cordial to him. He knew them from their forays into his areas of the kitchen, the dishwashing station and, more recently, the cooking areas.

Cleaning the restaurant was a grind. Bathrooms to be swabbed, carpets vacuumed, decks swept and tile mopped. Every seat and every table had to be sanitized and then the grand finale. The servers moved about filling salt and pepper, sweetener caddies and condiment holders. They cleaned the coffee urns and drinks stations, then set up the supplies of clean glasses and cups for the next shift.

While the servers were cleaning, the designated person was washing and drying napkins in the laundry room. Spot remover was used and each cleaned napkin was inspected and laid flat to prevent wrinkling.

When all the other chores had been finished, they gathered around a single table and sat to fold napkins into the signature COC fold. It was like a little party, without hors d'oeuvres. They gossiped and joked as their fingers flew.

"Paul. Did you learn rule number one?"

"What's that?"

"Never go anywhere in the dining room with empty hands. If your tables are clean pick up someone else's dirty dishes. Thank you very much." There were several hundred napkins to fold and the kitchen crew had left and the kitchen was dark when they folded and put away their last napkins, clocked out, and locked the back door.

As they clocked out they had to declare their tips. "Paul. Make up a number. I'm putting down $65.00. Put anything you want but keep it low."

"Okay." Paul agreed. He wrote $45.00 and would consider what to do next time when he was less tired.

Paul had a new respect for the servers. He had really worked as hard as he could to keep up with a few tables. His efficiency had risen a little with each experience and he hoped to be asked again. He had not counted his tips during the evening but, when he was alone in his bunk, he found that he had $130.00 in cash. He was stunned – this was much better than washing dishes or cooking. He determined to ask Peter to use him again – anytime!

With his head and heart full of the summer's memories, and as fall morphed into winter, Paul packed his stuff and left for Alabama. He had sold his canoe and other gear at the Guest Appreciation Festival and was comforted by the bulge of cash buttoned into his shirt pocket.

His earnings had exceeded his expectations and he was in love with the restaurant and food service business. He mulled his future and decided that he'd like to do it again. Peter and the GM had given him good reviews and he was assured of a job there again in the spring,

MIAMI, NOVEMBER 1999

What the hell is it all about? mused Paul. His 22nd birthday was coming and he was moping around the house in Huntsville. There were a few chores to keep him busy, but no construction work with his dad. Business was slow and Dad was looking for projects. His big project was painting the upstairs bedrooms. The COC season was over too quick he thought. His life was not mapped yet and he envied those who knew where they were going.

He had been working the phones trying to get in touch with Irene and his paddling buddy Marvin, both in Florida. He reached Marvin first.

"Paul! Damn it's good to hear your voice. How ya doin?" Are you at COC? Tell me everything."

"Me too buddy. I'm in Huntsville with my mom and dad and wishing I was on the river. I'll be going back in the spring as a cook at Corney's Cavern Restaurant. Tell me about yourself."

Marvin was back in Miami where he and Susan had met and married. They were both working in the Marriott Hotel kitchen as cooks then and had migrated to COC after experiencing whitewater sports there while on vacation in 1995. Now Susan's mother was ill and they had returned to help her. Marvin was cooking at the Marriott again and Susan stayed at home to tend to the kids and her mother.

"We won't be able to go back to COC for a while. Maybe never old pal." He told Paul where he was working.

"The Marriott!" That's where my friend Irene Linnick works. On Brickell Avenue. She's at the front desk. Do you know her?"

"Sure. I see her every day. I'll say hello to her for you." Before they hung up they hatched a plan for Paul to visit them in Miami. Marvin's mother-in-law had a house with plenty of room for a guest and Paul couldn't wait to hang up, pack and hit the road.

He called the hotel to see if he could talk to Irene and was not disappointed.

"Paul! How are you? Hold a minute while I switch phones."

She picked up an extension in the office and kicked back, anxious to hear about Paul's summer at COC.

He explained about Marvin's offer and she was suitably excited,

"Paul. It'll be so good to see you. How long will you stay?"

"It depends. I could be talked into a long-term visit. It depends on you Irene and on the situation at Marv's house. I don't want to be a pain but wouldn't it be wonderful to reacquaint?"

"Yeah. Sure. Thing is though Paul, I have a boyfriend. To tell you the truth I'm living with someone." There was a long silence on the line as Paul digested the news.

"I broke my abstinence vow and I think I'm in love. Pablo is Cuban and a very nice guy. I think you two will hit it off but I still want to see you if you're game."

"Well sure Irene," he said. You are a friend and not just a woman. I'll try to be good. I want to see you too."

The drive to Miami was not difficult. He used the interstates. Birmingham, Atlanta, Jacksonville, Miami. Paul didn't need a map until he got to Miami. He had lots of time to think about what he was doing now and where his life was heading. It made him a little sad and embarrassed to be on his own so much. He felt best at COC where work and play were engaging. He was proud, even though he knew it was silly, of his abilities with the Hobart. He'd never be unemployed. It was a start.

He recognized his mixed feelings about women. He wanted sex, of course, but he felt that he'd had bad luck with each of his girlfriends. He had not been totally serious when he told Irene that he would be celibate too but, in fact, he just had not found the right woman at the right time. His attitude toward Irene's announcement was sadness. Not surprise – she was just too lively to be good.

He used his sleeping bag in a rest area under the camper top amid a litter of paddling gear and other possessions. He arrived in Miami late on a Sunday morning. His good jacket and dress wear were on a hanger but he was basically a tee shirt and jeans guy. The weather was warm – just right. No cold and no tropical heat. He had thought it would be hotter.

Paul's long hair was tied in a tight ponytail and he used an electric razor to keep his beard short. Easy maintenance he thought. He was, in fact, a man to be reckoned with, but his cheerful countenance, good manners and ready smile made him instantly welcome everywhere. He did not see himself this way however. He felt somewhat unsure of himself - always ready to learn, but a little shy.

Marvin and Susan were living in Little Havana a few blocks south of *Calle Ocho*. The house was a 50's era CBS with a tile roof. It was on a large corner lot with tall tropical trees. An enormous hedge and vine covered walls and fences made it seem like an oasis in the modest, mixed neighborhood. The towers of downtown Miami loomed over the neighborhood trees. One could easily walk to stores on 8th and 9th Streets. There were apartment buildings on many streets.

After greetings and introductions at the door, Marvin opened the gate to let Paul park on the concrete apron of the separate garage. The kids, Mars, seven, and Sally, two-and-a-half, were excited to have company. Paul had seen them at COC but they had not had any real contact. Over the next few days he learned that he liked kids and that they were fun to play with and teach. Sally was in preschool, Mars in 2nd grade.

He later learned Susan's father had remodeled the garage into an apartment for Susan before she moved away from home. He lined his truck up neatly between a sharp old Chevrolet Impala and Marvin's old VW bus that he remembered from COC days.

"This neighborhood is safe but the folks here carry a cultural desire to bar windows and lock gates. It's from childhood memories in old Cuba. The bars work, of course, but they're really decorative."

"Ah. I see. What kinds of trees are these Marv?"

"We have tangerine, mango, avocado and limes. The Cubans say *limon* when they want a lime. Oranges are *naranjas*. Those big leaves growing in the corner are banana trees.

"We have to chop the bananas down every time, after we get a crop. A big new plant will come up in a few months. We have fruit coming out of our ears just now. It's wonderful," Marvin grinned, rubbing his belly.

He learned that Susan's mother, Carmen Alonso, a widow, was Cuban and that the local language was half Spanish and half English. They called it Spanglish.

"Call me Carmita. Por favor. Welcome to my house. *Mi casa es su casa.*" Susan's mom was a slender woman about his mom's age, late forties or early fifties. She kissed him on both cheeks and drew him instantly into the family circle.

They sat in the living room watching the two children play and Susan, fixing dinner, moved in and out of the room. She declined Paul's offer of assistance and said, "Later Paul. You can help clean up. You have guest status for the next 45 minutes. Then you're part of the family. You'd better make friends with my children and my mom."

"Just relax and enjoy it bud," advised Marvin. "There's plenty to do and you can help.

“Carmita is in chemo therapy and can’t work much. The grass grows every day and we need to put rice on the table.

“By the way. Irene said ‘Hi. Come and see me.’

“What is the plan Paul?”

“Thanks. We were really good friends and I can’t wait to see her again.”

“She told me to tell you come on over to the Marriott for lunch tomorrow if you can. You can either eat in the restaurant there or in the staff dining room. I’d recommend the restaurant. Or I could I’ll pack a lunch for you and make you brown-bag it. You can call her there now if you want.”

Paul did want. He got her on the phone and he spent the next few minutes letting Irene know that he’d buy her lunch the next day.

“Paul. I want you to meet Pablo. He is the kitchen manager here at the Marriott and I’ve told him all about your big adventures.”

“Not so big maybe,” said Paul shyly. “I want to meet him.”

Paul was glad he’d worn his go-to-court outfit, jacket and slacks, shirt and shoes. Irene was more beautiful than ever – she made her Marriott-prescribed business suit look like high couture. Only her nametag identified her as an employee. They embraced in the lobby then sat in lounge chairs, waiting for Pablo to join them at 1 PM. The lobby was richly paneled and formal in a very comfortable way. The air was cool and it seemed an oasis from the energetic bustle of Miami. Paul told her about his shifting work pattern at COC. “I thought I wanted to be a cook. It was hard work and a little more interesting than washing dishes, but now I love being a server. I doubled my income and, after a few more months as a waiter I think I could fit in at any restaurant.

"It just started as a job to be near the whitewater paddling but I now feel like I have another skill set that would work just about anywhere.

"Construction too. I think I would hate college. I learn so much every day in the working world."

"Me too Paul. I studied for my degree and it got me in the door here. But, honestly, I think I could have done without it. I spend my days learning about Marriott systems and culture. They're very good about developing staff… Oh here comes Pablo."

Pablo was taller than Paul. He looked well tanned and appeared heavy in the arms and chest, with an athlete's build and grace. He was wearing an open collared white shirt under a nice, Marriott style suit. The damp, dirty, white apron didn't quite match. He moved towards them quickly, gave Irene a peck on the lips and drew Paul's handshake into a bro-hug. He felt very strong to Paul but his manner was brilliantly sunny and friendly. "Good to meet you Paul. Irene talked about you so much I feel as though I know you."

Paul gave him his best smile and said, "*Mucho Gusto Pablo.*"

"Oh*! Hablas Espanol*! *No me digas. Eres otro Cubano*?"

"No. No. Just kidding. I have a Cuban friend I'm visiting who taught me to say, 'how do you do?'"

They all laughed at Paul's humor.

“Pablo,” Irene’s voice rose an octave as she said his name, “Do you know that you’re wearing an apron?”

Pablo looked down and removed the garment in question. “Oh I forgot. I was helping out in the kitchen and I had to run to meet you.” He removed the apron and walked it over to a desk clerk and asked him to send it to the laundry.

They walked to the dining room. It was cool and quiet with a pretty view of the palm fringed pool and gardens. Biscayne Bay glimmered in the background.

They talked about working in the hotel and about Paul’s experiences at COC .

Pablo was 28 years old and had just recently been promoted to Kitchen Manager. The hotel had 3 restaurants and banquet facilities that served hotel guests and meetings. Room service was still another dimension. “I’ve been here for 3 years. I started as a cook and worked in every position. I managed the poolside bar and grill, then the coffee shop and later on, as situations unfolded, I became the banquet manager and, after that, the main restaurant manager. Each of these facilities has its own manager but the main kitchen serves them all. Now as Kitchen Manager I have a much different set of challenges. Today I’m very challenged; two line cooks are out ill and the dishwasher didn’t show.

“I’m going to have to eat fast, but you two take as much time as you like.” He glanced at his watch.

“And. By the way, this meal is on the house. My job requires that I eat in every day and I am encouraged to have guests. My treat.”

They thanked him and enjoyed the food. Irene got a fancy salad and Paul the best hamburger he’d ever eaten.

Pablo had a shrimp bisque soup and a toasted cheese sandwich.

"Paul. What are your plans? Are you moving to Miami?"

"No big plan. I can stay as long as I like but I'm committed to returning to the Caverns Outdoor Center in the spring. I want to wait on tables next season. I've had a lot of kitchen experience."

"Really." Pablo looked keenly at Paul. "I don't suppose that you could consider working here for a while?

"We're so in the weeds. If you could even start today I'd be thrilled to have you."

"Well. I'd have to call home first then get my knives from my truck."

Pablo gave him a big grin. "Irene. This is karma. You have brought Paul here at a time when he could do us the most enormous favor."

"Glad to help. I've got to get back to the desk now. You boys talk and do what you need to do.

"Paul. I hope you will stay forever." She gave him a hug and a kiss on his face. Very near his lips. He felt a drop of her moisture on the corner of his mouth and was very affected by this show of friendship. He was jealous of Pablo and at the same time very glad that two such beautiful people could find their happiness together.

"Me too. See ya later."

"Pablo. I'd be happy to help. Could you help me make a phone call to the house?"

"Of course. Let's go to my office."

They went through a staff-only door and instantly entered a different world. The wall finishes were utilitarian, the floors linoleum tile, and the doors painted metal with aluminum kick plates. The long, wide hallway led them past offices with signs marked with their functions. Accounting. Finance. Executive Suite. Event Planning. Foodservice. Human Resources.

"Paul. I assume you are human?" Pablo joked. "Let's stop in here a moment and get you registered."

Paul was introduced to a young woman working in Human Resources, Patricia Cross. "Patty. This is Paul Hunter. He's clocking in today. Just as soon as you can get him signed in at $12.50 an hour. Use Irene Linnick, Marvin Smith, and me as references. He'll need a chef's pants, jacket and toque. Issue him work shoes as well. Okay?"

It was okay, so Pablo left them, asking Patty to bring him to the kitchen as soon as she could. "Quick Patty. We're dying in there and Paul may save us." It did not escape Paul's notice that Patty was about his age and that she had very blond hair and was pleasingly well rounded. A very pretty woman. Her hair was very shiny and pulled back into a neat bun. Her skin was fair and freckles were visible under transparent makeup of some kind. She was very kind to Paul and he admired her efficiency and professionalism as she explained various elements of the hire process. She gave him Marrriott new-employee literature in a manila envelope.

It had taken Pat over an hour to get him into the system, uniform him, and give him a lightning tour of the back of the house. He had been introduced to a number of people including the General Manager. The GM was cordial and told him that he had started with Marriott as a bellman in Salt Lake City, Utah.

Paul made a quick trip to his truck to get his kitchen toolkit and change in the men's locker room. They had given him 3 complete uniforms. H could have them cleaned in the house laundry as necessary.

The kitchen was vast; much larger than COC. It was the biggest kitchen he'd ever seen. Patty led him to a door marked MANAGER. Paul was surprised to see Pablo and Marvin in earnest conversation. Pat left him at the door.

Marvin glanced up and was astonished. "Boy. That was fast. Fine looking outfit." They were now dressed in identical checkered pants, leather shoes, white chef's jackets and sported tall toques on their heads.

He was given a training schedule that involved a lunch meeting with different managers every Wednesday. He would be one of ten new employees learning about the company. Paul was impressed.

"Marvin will be your mentor Paul. He'll give you an overall tour of the kitchen from the receiving dock to the grease pits. We have many different stations and we'll get you through them all before we finish. I hope you like it." Pablo was tying on a fresh apron. "I myself will be doing dishes until 6 o'clock. Ciao."

Marvin handed him a list of the workstations he'd be assigned to for the next 30 days for OJT: Fried Chicken, Cold Prep, Prime Rib, Desserts, Cook Station Number 1 - Vegetables, Cook Station Number 2 - Deep Fryer, Line Cook, Sanitation, and Expediting. He would also work Receiving at the loading dock, in Cooler Organization, in the Employee Lunchroom and on the Room Service Table.

"Marvin. I didn't expect to even look for a job here in Miami. I'm on vacation. Pablo begged me to help and I couldn't say no."

"Paul. You're such a slut."

Marvin started Paul at the fried chicken station explaining the system and the environment. "We have fried chicken on every menu: main dining room, coffee shop, pool snacks, and room service. It's all cooked right here. There is a special part of a big refrigerator reserved for covered, white, 55-gallon plastic barrels on wheels. Chicken parts are marinated in them for at least 12 hours. The barrels are rolled to the fryer station and the chicken, 40 pieces at a time, are dipped out and allowed to drain, dusted with a coating and pressure fried." Marvin showed Paul how to handle the big chicken dipper used to get the birds out of the barrel. He showed Paul 3 pressure fryers joined together. They were table height and their kettles each held about 40 pieces of chicken. The adjoining breading station had a steel mesh pan for draining, dusting and staging chicken parts close to the fryers.

"We use 3 or 4 barrels of chicken a day. More if there is a banquet. Your job at this station is to open boxes of chicken parts, breasts, leg quarters, thigh pieces and such. Wash and inspect them, trim off bits you would not want to eat. Maintain good sanitation at all times. There should be at least 4 full barrels when your shift is over.

"Dump a packet of marinade powder in a clean barrel, half fill it with water, and then put in as many cases of chicken as will fit. When the marinade water rises to the full mark, stop putting the chicken in. Stick a time label the barrel and roll it into the reefer.

When a barrel is empty, wheel it to the floor drain and use the built in bottom spigot to drain the liquid. Wash and sanitize the barrel to get it ready for another batch." There was a carton opening station with double sinks to wash the birds. A box of rubber gloves stood at the ready to keep hands out of the chicken mess.

"Meanwhile, like a chicken with its head cut off, you will be dipping the marinated chicken parts out onto a drain rack, breading it, frying it and moving the finished product to the holding ovens."

He showed Paul the pressure fryers full of hot oil. "Drop your 40 pieces, gently, 4 at a time. Close the pressure lid and set the timer for 12 minutes. Got it?"

"Sure. It looks like fun. Lots of fun."

They looked into the holding ovens and found only 1 hotel pan heaped with delicious looking fried chicken. There was a wire rack on the bottom of the pan to keep the product from sitting in a puddle of oil. The pieces had a good brown and were crisp and fresh looking.

"Paul. We gotta hurry buddy. Let's get to frying us some chicken and loading this holding unit up. Serious dinner hour starts in 2 hours and you have to get it on." He showed Paul how to coat 40 pieces of chicken into a basket and drop them into the hot fat and close the pressure lid and set the timer.

"I'll come back and check on you after a while. I'm gonna cut some vegetables." He saw Paul frown and recognized a set of concerns. "Don't fret bud. You'll get the hang of this in one day and we'll move you to another station tomorrow or the next day. There are about 20 work stations to master. When you get 'em all you'll have a better appreciation of how we feed thousands of people a day, 24 hours a day, 7 days a week. We are scheduled to work until 10PM. We'll keep you busy.

"I'll show you how to filter the oil and clean up later."

Paul managed to get the holding oven filled to his spec sheet and found the work hard and not so interesting. It was so one-note.

He reflected on his wage of $12.50 an hour. It seemed fairly high but he had no standards to go by. He got $6.00 an hour at COC plus tips. This Marriott work paid enough to start.

Paul received visits from Pablo and Irene in the course of the shift as well as regular contact with Marvin. He had dinner with the 3 of them in the staff dining room. He enjoyed a taste of his own fried chicken. The price was modest for staff. He could even charge it against his paycheck. Pretty damn good chicken he thought.

He learned a lot on his first day. In the days following he also learned how to cold prep vegetables of all varieties, cook massive quantities of mashed potatoes, steam vegetables, roast prime ribs and even work on the line where the action was best. He liked his job and thought that he was building a skill set for life at COC and afterwards.

Marvin approached him with a deal before the first week was up. Paul had expressed a desire to get an apartment in the neighborhood because he didn't want to wear out his welcome.

"Paul. Stay in the garage apartment and take your meals with us. We can work the same shift and either drive or walk to work together – it's only a mile away. We'll give you a terrific deal on rent. Say $155.00 per week including utilities and board. *Todas las comidas* you care to eat." Paul was learning a little Spanglish every day. "What do you say? *¿Que dice?"*

Paul didn't answer for a moment because he was so happy to be wanted.

Marvin jumped in again, "We all like having you around and it will help Carmita. She gets social security from my father-in-law's death benefits but Medicare won't kick in for a few years. She gets Medicaid benefits, from Uncle Sam thank you, but she needs more to keep this house going. That's why we're here.

"That, and the fact that she loves having us around. Especially the kids. She says they bring life into the house."

"Ah Marvin. That would be great but you have to promise me something."

"What?"

"We have got to have a 3-way conversation with me and Susan to promise me to let me know if any of that changes. I don't need the job really, the money is not a big issue, but I like the idea of learning more about the hospitality business. I want to be a pro like you and Pablo. I believe that I'm going back to COC in the spring.

"And I'm having a great time. Here in Florida it's so different. I feel like I'm visiting another country."

"*No problema hermano*. Let's have that talk now."

Paul's new digs were very pleasing to him. The garage space was now a 450 square foot efficiency apartment with a bathroom and walk in closet. The garage doors had been left on but were just a sham and not functional – Carmita and her husband did not want to get a building permit. Taking down the doors would have tipped off any inspector in the area.

Inside, the garage doors were concealed by a properly built and insulated sheetrock wall with decorative wainscoting. The curtains were not too girly and there were landscapes and family pictures on the walls. HVAC included a ceiling fan and a through-the-wall, reverse cycle, air conditioner. Neither heating nor cooling were needed at this time of year. A love seat, a recliner chair, a double bed, a bathroom and a walk-in closet provided most of the comforts Paul needed. He needed less than 6 inches of hanger space. There was bedding and towels but no TV.

Paul thought having his own space was fabulous.

Windows provided cross ventilation and nice views of the tropical back yard. "Marvin. Would you all mind if I got a TV and cable set-up?"

"Not at all. Let's call our cable company and see if we can just add you on. Shouldn't cost much."

Paul made a beeline to the nearest Sears store and returned with a mammoth box containing a 32" screen television set. The first piece of home furnishing he ever bought.

The weather was beautiful in Miami and they walked to work most days. Virtually every shop and advertisement they saw was in Spanish. Conversations on the street were in Spanish or, sometimes, Spanglish. People seemed lively, happy and busy.

"The Cubans are hustlers Paul. They work hard and play hard and try to live the good life.

"I grew up in the Southwest section of Miami in an American neighborhood that gradually became all Cuban. The natives all moved to the suburbs. My father was in his early twenties in 1960 when Castro came into power and the middle class Cubans fled to the US - mostly Miami. He said that the area we call Little Havana now, was going downhill fast. The shops along the main streets were all empty. People preferred driving to the malls and local merchants all went broke. It was a disaster.

"Most of the Cubans who came here were poor. They had to leave a lifetime of material accumulations behind. They had no money, no houses or furniture, no jewelry and no jobs. Coming here was a leap into the unknown for them.

"The government helped them a lot but more than that, they helped themselves. They began to open little shops selling the goods and services they were used to at home. And restaurants. They revitalized the whole area. Miami is way up on other cities with respect to having people living close to the city center.

"Now, 4 decades later their kids are voting republican and are more educated and professional than most of the rest of America."

They stopped for a Cuban coffee and pastry most days. "*Un cafe´ y un pastelito por favor*." Paul loved ordering and the people behind the counters enjoyed hearing his American accent. They appreciated his attempts. They ate their *pastelitos* and drank their coffee standing at the counter. If other customers appeared they'd move a few feet and lean against the building.

Paul reluctantly called his mother to declare that he would be away for Christmas. She said she understood but he could tell that she was disappointed. "Mom. I'm learning so much here. And I'll be sending you money every week.

"Do you or Dad need money?"

"No honey. Thanks for asking. Dad and I are doing all right. We just need a Paul-fix once in a while. Call me every week. Okay."

"Okay. Love to Dad. I love you too."

Paul learned everything he wanted and needed to know about frying large quantities of chicken in 2 days and went on to the hot vegetable station.

He learned how to create tons of sweetly delicious, skin-on, mashed potatoes in the big Hobart mixer using cream, butter, grated Parmesan cheese, salt and pepper. He steamed fresh green vegetables that others had prepped and, following his script, kept the holding cabinets filled to a prescribed level, gradually cutting back as the dinner hour slowed and then ended. Room service, coffee shop and poolside needs were lighter than the main dining room.

His paycheck was directly deposited to a new bank account and, to his surprise, the bank offered him a Master Card. He accepted it, activated it and left it in his wallet. He thought that he might use it sometime but he was so used to paying cash and having no monthly bills that he was leery of credit.

Paul had no social life outside of his new family and a few acquaintances at work. He was eager to make friends and took every opportunity to chat it up at work. Because there was an older guy in the kitchen also named Paul. They began calling Paul 'Hunter' at work.

The slightly grizzled Paul I chatted with Paul as they worked side-by-side prepping vegetables. Hunter felt like a pro using his own knives.

"Hunter. I'm lucky to be here. I just got an early release from prison. I got caught doing something really stupid. I broke into a grocery store and stole cash from the registers. About $400.00, I think.

"The reason I don't know is that I didn't have time to count it. They busted me as I went out the back door. I got 2 years but only had to serve 9 months."

"Oh my God Paul. I'm sorry for your problems. I guess I've done worse than that myself. Stupidly. But I didn't get caught."

"You were lucky Hunter. Prison was for shit. The only thing is that it got me clean of cocaine. That was my main problem and I rehabbed in jail. I guess I did good. And it wasn't my first crime – only the one I got caught for."

This conversation played over again in Paul's mind many times. He thought back to the thievery and mischief that he and Mitch had gotten away with and wondered why they were so blessed. He'd seen pain and trouble in Paul I's eyes. He was glad his wayward childhood was behind him.

Paul attempted something very scary 10 days before Christmas. He called Patricia Cross while on his break and said, "Hi Pat. This is Paul Hunter. Do you remember me?"

"Yes, of course Mr. Hunter. What can I do for you?"

"Well Pat. Call me Paul please or I'll think you're Cross."

She laughed at his little joke.

"Say Pat. I, uh. I mean," He stammered a little, "Do you think you might like to see a movie and have dinner with me sometime?"

"Let's see. Yes!" she said. "Do you mean now?"

"Well yes. But I have to work tonight. Until ten. What nights are you off?"

"Weekends only I'm afraid."

"I'm free Sundays and Mondays. So Sunday then? What would you like to see? I haven't been to a movie in like forever so you pick and I can say I haven't seen it. I was thinking we could see *American Beauty* or *Toy Story II*. Pick One."

"American Beauty," she said immediately. "Where and when do you want to meet? By the way, call me Patty."

"Can I pick you up at your house Patty? I'm afraid I drive an old pick-up, but I promise it's clean. Almost clean anyway."

She gave him a Coral Gables address along with some complicated directions involving circles and streets with names instead of numbers. They agreed to a 5 o'clock time, dinner at the Versailles Restaurant, then 8 o'clock show time near the restaurant.

Paul was excited and he thought that Patty sounded pleased. When Sunday came, he spent a great deal of time grooming for his date. He followed his high school rules. Shower, shave, masturbate, brush and floss. He wore his only jacket, slacks and clean loafers.

Her apartment was on the 2nd floor of a tired old building. It was in a middle class neighborhood at the edge of an opulent district of beautiful homes and estates. He climbed dark, narrow stairs to knock on the door of 201. He heard her footsteps and the door unlatching.

When Paul saw what Patty wore he thought he should have jerked off twice. She was very fetching in a scoop neck, white peasant blouse and form fitting jeans. She wore fuck-me red shoes. The outfit was topped off with a red, Spanish style shawl. Her hair was different.

"Hey Paul. Come in for a minute. We have plenty of time"

The corner apartment was neat and plainly furnished. There was a Formica table with two kitchen chairs, a sofa and 2 easy chairs. Her bed was tucked behind the couch. The minimal kitchen did not take up much room. It was a 1950's efficiency with a combination bathroom and closet. She had it fixed up with bright curtains and pillows on the chairs and couch.

The walls were somewhat crowded with travel posters from France, Italy and Spain. Filmy curtains fluttered at the windows. The through-the-wall air conditioning unit was off in the mild evening.

"My God Patty. This place is so much like mine. I'm living in Marvin's family's garage apartment. I like your posters better than my pictures. Where'd you get them?"

"Thank you sir. I got them here and there. All over actually - if you like I'll take you shopping one day soon.

"Gimme a few seconds." She stepped into the bathroom without closing the door, and leaned toward a mirror to expertly apply and blot lipstick and give her hair a fluff. She turned out the bathroom light and they left the apartment for their date.

They were apparently in the landing and takeoff zone of the Miami International Airport. Several jets roared overhead while they were there. "Sorry Paul. I'm used to the noise now, but, because of the jet noise, the rent is very low here.

He led the way down the stairs offering his arm to give her support as she negotiated the stairs in high heels.

Paul was so proud of his date. He held the door while she settled in the truck and made her wear her seat belt. He drove gently through the beautiful Coral Gables streets as she directed him back to *Calle Ocho* and S.W. 36th Avenue.

This was the first real Cuban dinner restaurant Paul had been in. He knew he liked the *comidas* that Susan and Carmita provided and the *café* and *pastilitos* that he and Marvin had been eating. But this restaurant was amazing. It was plain and fancy at the same time. It had a neighborhood vibe and fancy mirrors on every wall with world class Cuban food. The place was very busy but they were seated quickly in a mirrored back room. The background babble was entirely in Spanish as far as Paul could tell.

The waitress bid them *buenas noches* and offered them a choice of Spanish or English menus. They chose one of each. Pat ordered the house special salad. "I've got to watch my figure or you won't," she flirted. Paul had *masas de puerco fritas.* They shared Galician White Bean Soup as an appetizer.

Paul wondered why he kept thinking 'best ever.' The soup was super. Best ever, he thought again. His pork chunks, fried sweet plantains and black beans were wonderful. Patty's salad was beautifully made. He realized then that Cuban food and Mexican food were not the same. Mex, as he knew and loved it, had the heat of peppers and the richness of coriander lurking in every bite. Cuban food was well seasoned with lots of garlic but no sharp edges or bite. It was heavenly.

They took their time with dinner since they had 3 hours to go and just a few miles to the theater. They talked about childhood memories from Huntsville - him, and Long Island, New York - her. Patty was 23, on her own for over a year, and thrilled to be working at the great hotel chain. "My goal is to become competent in Spanish. I need it to apply for a post in Spain. The company will give me a Spanish test when I think I'm ready. Soon. I've had courses in Hotel Management and I have had experience in a few smaller American chains."

Paul gave her his work history and she was suitably amazed when he got to the Barbecue Shack episode.

"Holy Mackerel! You must have been scared."

"A little bit. It wasn't half as scary as calling you however."

They laughed.

After their Cuban coffees and flan dessert she said, "Paul. I'm so full. What would you think about taking a walk before the movie?"

"I'd love it. Can you really walk in those heels?"

"Girl Scouts are always prepared," she smiled at him as she reached into her ample purse and removed a pair of flat shoes. "The red shoes are for show. Attitude, you know. These booties are made for walking."

They strolled a block down *Calle Ocho,* AKA S.W. 8th Street, then went south on Douglas Road, AKA S.W. 37th Avenue to Miracle Mile, AKA Coral Way. Downtown Coral Gables' fancy shops were decorated for Christmas. Patty held Paul's arm as they moved along window-shopping for things they didn't need or want. "God. I love looking at this stuff," said Patty. Maybe I'll buy some of it when I grow up."

They discussed Christmas plans and discovered that they were working 2nd shift, she at the front desk, he, and Marvin, in the kitchen as usual.

The company had asked for volunteers to allow employees with families to get Christmas day off. Marvin said his kids wouldn't miss him after they opened their presents. He and Paul would start work by 1 o'clock on Christmas day.

On impulse Paul invited Patty to spend Christmas morning with his new family at *la casa.* He knew them well enough to know that they would rejoice at having her with them.

When the time came to hike back to his car for the movie she said, "Paul. I've had such a good time. I like being with you. Would you mind skipping the movie? I'd like to walk back to my place and have a night cap."

Paul felt a little woozy thinking about what she might mean. Her words had been a little slow and sort of breathy. "Of course. Lead on." He took her hand. It felt so natural and they walked a mile or so back to her place.

It turned out that the nightcap was a glass of water since she had no booze.

Afterwards he held her in his arms and she began crying. "Oh Paul. I'm sorry I did this to you. I feel like such a slut. I'm so lonely and it just felt so good to be with you." They were sated with sex and with passionate kissing. Wrapped together in her sheet they sat on the couch and cuddled, drinking from the same glass.

She knew that he would be leaving in March. She ventured, "Paul. I'm about ready for my Spanish test and I think I'll leave in the spring. If I can't get to Spain I'll try for New York.

"Like I said, I'm kinda lonely here. I have a few girlfriends but no men friends. Would you consider being my Sunday boyfriend for a few months?"

"Hm. Let me think. Yes." He got his arm under her and turned her so that he could plant a good kiss on her soft mouth. She opened her lips and they were soon back in her bed.

When they were resting he said, "Patty. I'm going to get you a little Christmas present tomorrow." He looked at his watch. "I mean later today so that you'll have something to open next Sunday. I'm doing my Christmas shopping tomorrow, I mean today." It was after midnight. I need something for my folks, for my brother Mitch and for Marvin and Susan's family.

"Say Patty, it's getting late. Can I spend the night with you?"

She answered by setting her clock for 6:30 and turning off the bed lamp. "Paul. If you try to leave I'll hurt you."

He laughed and they snuggled until they slept. Both were tired from the emotional coupling and togetherness they felt.

Paul had a wonderful Monday morning. He attacked Patty when the alarm went off and they made love before the sun peeked in the window.

He washed her in the shower enjoying her luscious body. Each breast, pointy and pneumatic, got kissed, suckled, washed and hand rinsed. He did not miss anything, including the ticklish bottoms of the feet. "Paul. I've never had such a bath."

"Me neither," he said as she began to work on his body.

When he became aroused, somewhere between his toe scrub and shampoo, she said, "Not again Paul. My heart is ready but my other organs are done for the day."

"Me too, but the next time I see this beautiful body I want to count the freckles."

After their incredible shower she was rushed to be on time for work. "Paul. Do you need a ride to your car?"

"No. Thanks Patty. I want to walk my mind back to earth. Have a great day. See ya at work Tuesday."

They walked down the stairs, she to roar off downtown and he to hike through the beautiful neighborhoods to *Calle Ocho* and get his vehicle. He drove to Dadeland Mall and bought Christmas gifts.

Paul found the UPS store and sent his store-wrapped gifts to his parents and Mitch and Molly – they all went to Huntsville where they would celebrate the holidays without him for the first time. The season was not without sadness on that account.

Christmas morning was a party. Patty came at 8 AM. with wrapped toys for the kids, a tea set for Carmen, matching hats, watch-cap style, for Marvin and Susan. Paul gave her a Hermes scarf.

"Oh Paul. This is too much! You shouldn't have spent so much." She handed him a long thin package that turned out to be a walking stick that unscrewed into two pieces for storage and travel. It had a built-in compass on top and a knife in the hollow handle.

Susan and Carmita had not met Patty before this day. They gave every sign of approval for Paul's guest. Patty was delighted to be a part of the family.

While Marvin and the other women set out the lunch, and the kids played with their new treasures, Patty sat close to Paul on the couch taking it all in. "Thank you for having me here," she whispered. This was wonderful. By the way." She sat even closer and hugged his bicep. "You can unwrap your big present at my place after work tonight."

"With pleasure Patty. It'll be late. But tomorrow's Sunday and we can stay in bed all day." Paul leaned in close and whispered into her ear, "By the way, next Friday is my birthday…" She growled at him and the kids looked up expectantly, thinking that they might be about to fight.

Susan stepped into the room singing, "Come and get it lovebirds. Y'all can clean up after we eat. You've lazed around long enough."

JANUARY 2000

Patty passed her Spanish test and was offered a 1-year employment contract by Marriott in Malaga, Spain at the A. C. Palacio Hotel. She would start in reception and perhaps be rotated into other areas of the operation.

Paul was very happy for Patty but he saw that the end of their idyllic relationship was near at hand. He hosted a farewell dinner for her involving Irene, Pablo, Marvin and Susan. They ate in a small private dining room at the Versailles Restaurant and presented her with a little electronic translating device. It handled several major European languages.

Patty started her adventure with a visit tol her parents in New York on the 15th of February. Her car was already sold and Paul gave her a lift to the airport. "I boxed my stuff and UPS'd it to New York. I won't be taking much to Spain. Mostly clothing and a few pictures. The company will give me a mentor to get a rental apartment and whatever I need for making the big change.

“I wish I could take you Paul.”

“Yeah. Me too Patty. But we have to part for now. Send me postcards. Okay?”

MARCH 2000

Paul was happy to be back on his river - the Clancy River - in the budding Georgia spring. He was in his secret garden on the riverbank out of sight. Quiet. Peaceful. Alone.

He sat erect in his kayak in the quiet water. His double-bladed paddle rested athwart ship on the gunwale. Paul was protected by his wet suit, basking in the noon sun with his eyes closed. Dreaming about his life. Experiencing wisps of memories, fears, sorrows and happiness.

He deliberately let his mind drift to the people who were important to him. Mom and Dad were in a special place providing a foundation for his emotional security and wellbeing.

Brother Mitch, his idol, had first gone to Asheville to be with Molly. He seemed to be heading in a direction Paul envied – toward stated and rational goals. Gone to make a life with his girlfriend – more than a girlfriend - Molly. They were living in Charlotte, North Carolina where they had bought a consignment, antique shop.

Sarah, his first love, had gone her way without him. Other women in his life, Irene and Patty were gone.

Some friends were gone forever. Megan, his boss, landlord and lover - Johnny, his lawyer. They were gone forever. The Barbecue Shack was gone.

Paul had spent a lot of time living alone in tents. Even now, living in staff housing, he felt slightly alienated from the COC culture. The hardcore, permanent employees were the athletes and experts in whitewater matters. The most prominent were past Olympic participants and the hopeful youths actively competing at a high level.

The hardcore whitewater people worked in Administration and Retail as well as serving as instructors and guides. A number of them were involved in the International Adventure Travel Department, making trips to far-away places like Nepal and Costa Rica. These elite folks tended to look down on foodservice workers.

The cooks, servers and other restaurant workers were mostly locals and summer-employed students. They were socially inferior to Olympic heroes and hopefuls.

Paul sensed patterns in his affairs. He wanted do-overs.

###

Hi Reader. Thanks for experiencing Paul Hunter's story with me. Go to the next page for a sample of *Hunter II*, next in the 3-part *Hunter* Series. Go to billserle.com or Amazon.com if you want to buy – please!

Bill Serle

Hunter II

A tale of love and crime

COC, MONDAY, APRIL 1, 2000

Dahlia Schmitt was a delight. Her pretty figure and boyish haircut caught Paul's eye on her second day at Caverns Outdoor Center. She seemed taller than her actual 5'4" because of her confident posture and long neck. She was in the United States on a work/study visa and she planned to be in the states for the summer.

The Outdoor Center seemed like a paradise to Dahlia when she'd first planned her visit from her home in Germany. She hadn't yet made friends with the women working at the center and felt shy about the men. Her English was good and getting better every day. As she bantered with the staff while bussing tables and taking her turn at the dishwashing station her accent and vocabulary improved. She missed her family in Berlin.

Archie Phillips, the restaurant manager, liked her but she spurned his advances, partly because he seemed too old for her, and partly because he thought he had a right to touch her when they spoke. He would put his hand on her arm or shoulder and it creeped her out. She was scared by the lust she saw in his eyes.

Paul was cooking when he first met Dahlia. When he became a waiter, he sometimes helped her with overflowing bus tubs, or crinkled his eyes as he held doors open for her. His beard was full and he had a ponytail. His hazel eyes were beautiful. He stood six feet tall and looked strong and solid. She jumped at the chance to get away from staff housing when he asked her to go rafting on her day off.

Paul was thrilled when she said, "Oh yah. Dat vould be nice." He loved her accent.

Paul did not like the way some people treated her as he often felt something of an outcast himself. He hoped to make a friend.

Archie, standing nearby, out of sight, overheard the invitation with displeasure. He marched off angry at Paul's success.

Paul reserved a boat for the next Monday. He ordered a two-person "Duckie," as they called the slender rafts propelled by double-bladed kayak paddles. He felt it would be more fun for a novice like Dahlia. He had taken the guide course the previous year and knew the Clancy River well. Sometimes he got work as a raft guide on his days off.

Monday, in the staff-housing washroom, he did his morning toilet with great care. He scissored and razored his beard to a fashionable buzz. His ponytail was pulled tight and his teeth were brushed and flossed. Clean shorts and a new tee shirt made him feel fashionable in the woodsy way. He donned his visor at a jaunty angle. He wore his neoprene river shoes.

There was no charge for employees as long as equipment was available. Guided rafting trips on the Clancy River cost clients forty dollars per person. They received their gear and attended a five minute safety lesson before riding to the put-in by bus, along with other guests and employees. Dahlia wore a pink baseball cap, shorts, tee shirt and sturdy Teva sandals. Paul thought she looked smashing.

The two boarded the bus for the put-in after donning wet suits. They carried their paddles and Paul's waterproof wet sack containing their clothing. The rubber suits were needed because summer heat had not yet set in. Paul had packed cool cokes, crackers, and apples for sustenance. Their deflated boat was on top of the bus along with the larger rafts and other duckies according to guests' choices when they signed up.

The drive was a bit over five miles on Route 72. They saw the Clancy River from time to time as it romped alongside their route. The pace was slow and the driver deliberate as they maneuvered along the winding road. The trip leader stood near the driver and regaled the passengers with funny stories, jokes, and river safety reminders. There was a lot of laughter and kibitzing.

Paul explained that the rapids they would traverse were Class I, II and III, in the parlance of the whitewater river sports authorities. Class I and II are mild and easy enough for even inexperienced boaters. Perhaps boring for hard-core paddlers. Class III requires a degree of skill and effort that may be within the limits of inexperienced but fit people. Class IV and V are increasingly challenging. Class VI is over the line - too dangerous for recreation.

The Clancy River was great fun for the thousands of people who ran it in rafts, kayaks and canoes each year. A hydroelectric dam controlled water levels on the river to provide appropriate flow for recreation and electric power at different times of day.

There were about forty people for the last trip of the day. Paul sat on the aisle next to Dahlia. Their shoulders pressed together as the bus made its turns on the forest road in the leaf-filtered sunlight. Paul felt a great peace in Dahlia's presence but she showed some apprehension about their upcoming adventure.

"Don't worry Dalia," Paul said.

"It vill be my first time on a river," she said quietly. "You vill have to show me how to do it."

"No problema. You'll love it. It is the most peaceful place on earth. We'll be close to nature but your wet suit and your PFD will keep you safe and warm. I know the river and I'm sure you will want to go again. I'll be happy to take you anytime."

She smiled up at him and felt a building trust. Her grayish blue eyes were clear and direct. He seemed so strong and sure of himself. "What's a PFD again?"

"A personal flotation device. PFD. Your life jacket."

"Oh, yah. I forgot the initials."

She liked the confident way Paul conducted himself. He did not swagger. His attitude was deferential and he accommodated everyone he encountered with a polite smile and strong eye contact.

The bus turned off into the raft staging area by the river called the put-in. The deflated boats were quickly unstrapped, lowered to the ground, and inflated by the put-in staff. Paul helped handle the boats as guests and guides formed into groups and departed on the water. Dahlia stood to one side holding their paddles. The number of people watching dwindled as rafts departed.

Dahlia and Paul were the last boat of the day. Paul planned a leisurely pace to make sure that Dahlia would not get too tired and to insure that they would be alone in the river world.

The shouts of the other boaters from their bus faded and the magic environment asserted itself. The sunlight was intermittent with great rocks and green forest on the banks. The air was still and cool and the mineral smell of clear water bubbling over river rocks added to a sense of change from land animals to river creatures.

The initial Class I and II rapids were interesting rather than frightening for the novice. She paddled as Paul directed, sometimes pulling forward with her twin blades, sometimes resting, and sometimes using a reverse stroke on one side or the other to help him steer around rocks.

Dahlia's seat in the bow of the boat was supremely comfortable. The inflatable boat's bottom was just a big long flat air cushion to make the boat self-bailing. The thwart was a firm backrest and the stiffly inflated sides rose to a comfortable height. The rubberized fabric of the craft was strong enough to resist the daily assault of shallow water and sharp rocks.

Her wet suit, PFD, and neoprene shoes made her feel like she was wearing a comfortable suit of armor. The dollops of water that splashed aboard as they progressed down the river did not discomfort her. The whole process was exciting.

Paul, in the stern, was alert to the flow of the river over its bottom and sides. There were many large rocks all around them and he picked their way through waves and rocks with respect for his passenger's enjoyment.

"There's Eddie's Bath Tub," Paul said.

She saw his paddle reach along the side of the boat to point at a huge rock ahead on their left side. The water noises grew loud as they approached and she could see the water curling around the giant boulder with great force. "What do you mean?" her voice quavered slightly with fright.

"That's where Eddie Minton's kayak got broken on the big rocks, just where the water moves the fastest. He had to bail out and swim in the whirlpool with a dislocated shoulder.

"Don't worry" he called out. "I know just where to enter the big eddy behind the rock. Let me paddle and you give me a big reverse stroke on the left side when I tell you. It's like a carnival ride. Raise your left hand. Yeah. That's the side you need to reverse when I tell you to do it."

They drew ever closer to the "Bath tub," and the roar of the water got louder. This was far bigger than the other rapids they'd experienced.

They moved faster and faster toward the maelstrom. She could feel Paul paddling hard. Then they went over a giant drop of rushing water as Paul yelled, "Now Dahlia. Hard left reverse!"

She dug her paddle in and the boat spun into a tight left turn into the calm water behind the rock. The boat bobbed quietly now and the river was really rushing by and was higher than the boat. They were nestled in the eddy that was like sort of a quiet hole in the water.

They both vocalized. "Wow!" "Yay!"

"Good job Dahlia. Was that fun?"

"Oh my God. It vas vonderful. Thank you for showing me. I feel that you saved my life. How is Eddie now? Did he recover from his injury?"

"Yeah. He's fine. Eddie is COC's head of accounting and he runs the river almost every day."

They ran several rapids and Dahlia grew more confident. Paul pulled to the shore at deserted Riverside Park. She wrestled her wet suit off to pee in the ladies room. It was a smelly wilderness toilet, like a big outhouse, but her empty bladder made her more comfortable and she looked forward to their next rapid as she buckled her PFD and helped paddle away from the shore.

Paul surprised her by steering for shore into a thicket of flowering bushes. "Bring your paddle up into the boat," he directed.

As the bow pushed into the bushes she realized that they were entering a hidden branch of the river. The trees were thinner here and transparent water revealed pebbles and green algae flowering just under the surface.

"Let's rest here a while," Paul said as he stood and stepped out of the boat into the shallows. He offered his hand to steady Dahlia as she stepped out of the boat next to him. She gave him a shy smile.

"This is the most beautiful spot I have ever seen."

The nearby river murmured. Bird songs trilled and the slight breeze was welcome. She spotted some blue and gold flowers at the edge of the water and stooped to get a better look.

Paul kneeled in the stream next to her and then sat back on his heels. "I like to come here. This is my favorite chilling spot. I don't think anyone else knows about it. This is the reason I love COC so much."

He splashed to the boat, dragged it to shore, and flipped it over. He sat on the boat and leaned back. He looked so comfortable that Dahlia wanted to join him. They lay on their backs quietly and took in the smells, sounds and sights around them. They did not talk at first and spent a quiet half hour. Their silence was warm and they both slipped into a light sleep with late afternoon sunlight brightening their eyelids.

After a time Paul said, "My parents live in Alabama. I have a brother living in Charlotte. His name is Mitch and he is doing very well. He owns and operates a second hand furniture and consignment store.

"I'm sorta the black sheep of my family. I save my salary and try to live simply. The money I get this season will last me all year. This is my second season at COC. I cooked all last year. Mostly on the line but sometimes I baked and did general cooking for clinics, staff and the daily specials. I liked working in the kitchen"

"Yes. I know about Charlotte. That's in North Carolina, yah? How long does it take to get to Alabama from here? How far is Alabama?" The cadence of her voice was slow as she formed the words into English from her native German.

"Huntsville is a 6 or 7 hour drive from here. It's even further from Charlotte to Huntsville. Do you have sisters and brothers?"

"No but I have a lot of cousins. Mostly on my father's side of the family. I am an only child. When I get home I hope to work for an airline. My English is good. Yes?"

"Very, very good," he replied. "Where did you go to school?"

"After high school I attended a hospitality school where we learned about hotel, restaurant and amusement company management. How about you?"

"I graduated from Huntsville High school four years ago. I did a lot of construction work as a laborer and carpenter in high school - mostly for my dad. I've done a lot of other jobs but guiding rafts is my favorite. I do it here at COC on my day off sometimes. Waiting on tables pays about the same but it's steady. Sometimes guides wait all day and don't get a trip. They make their money from tips too."

They were both twenty-two years old.

She nodded and they spoke intermittently, getting to know each other. She would have to leave the country in October to go back to her real life in Berlin.

She said that her mother was a "haus frau with lots of friends and community activities. Mine dad is an architect."

"Cool," said, Paul. My mom and dad both work. Mom sells insurance. She's a certified financial planner and gives investment advice. She is why I have money in the bank. Dad is in construction. Sometimes he's employed and sometimes he free lances. He let me help him every summer when I was in school, so I know a bit about carpentry and I can do plumbing and electric work too."

They returned to the river after a time and enjoyed the miles on the water, the solitude, and peaceful mountain scenery that unfolded around them. Paul never tired of it and Dahlia was beginning to love it.

Two weeks later, on their third trip down the river, they took 2 one-person duckies. Paul led and Dahlia followed him through the rapids. She felt empowered as she successfully managed her duckie. This was her first time in a boat alone. They pushed though the bushes to their secret spot, flipped their boats, removed their PFDs and flopped down to rest. They were hot and the sun was strong this day.

Dahlia was sweating and pulled down the big center zipper to expose some skin to the slight breeze and reclined. Paul, right next to her, unzipped his wet suit to the waist slipped his arms and torso free of the garment. He too lay back, facing her.

Her baseball cap was off, and he could see a slight sheen of sweat on her forehead. Her short hair looked a little spiky and damp in the warm air. He thought it gave her a pixie look.

Without thinking Paul reached out and touched her zipper. She looked hot. His finger lingered on the zipper and she looked at him with wide eyes. She licked her lips and he touched the zipper again with two fingers and ventured to lower it an inch more.

To their mutual surprise, she sat up and pulled the big zipper all the way down and slipped the garment half-off just as Paul had. Her beautiful breasts, freckled shoulders, and back were covered with goose bumps. To Paul she was the most amazing sight he'd ever seen.

Paul was not a virgin. He had girlfriends in high school and had first done the deed in the back of his prom date's Ford Explorer. The tailgate window was up and the back seats folded. They had spent a happy night rolled up in a comforter in the back of the truck. They'd broken up the next afternoon when he'd suggested a ride in the Explorer. Paul was not sure why she had blown him off but, gentlemen that he was, he took it like a man and never saw her again.

Dahlia lay back making no attempt to cover herself. She filled his eyes and then his hands as he began to stroke her smooth skin.

Her armpits were unshaved in the European fashion that many female COC employees followed. He saw that her body hair was sparse. She had never used a razor. Her leg fuzz was very soft and blond. They kissed gently at first then with rising passion as the intensity of their situation took hold of them.

She had been naked under the wet suit and they were soon rid of the heavy garments. She tugged at the damp waistband of his boxers and now they were together like Adam and Eve in a wilderness Garden of Eden. She noticed that Paul was a beautiful man in the nude. His body hair was dark and it accentuated the muscles of his chest and abdomen. Paul's skin and hair were soft to her touch.

They made love twice. Rough and quick the first time. After a rest, they entwined again and made love on top of her duckie with delicious care and deliberation.

Their kisses were passionate and their words breathless. "Oh Paul. This is vonderful. Ve are like a natural man and voman."

Paul murmured an assent and, in a few minutes, came up with a question. "Dahlia. What about, uh - protection. I mean you're not ready to get pregnant. Are you?" His voice rose slightly as he managed the question.

"Don't vorry Paul." Her accent was showing itself. "My mum gave me a supply of Morning After pill in case... You know, in case I made love mit somebody."

She smiled at him. "I never thought I vould need them. I'm not a virgin but I don't make love very often. Not for two years maybe." Paul fell in love.

Their stay in the secret garden was almost too long. The power company dam at the head of the river shut down at 8 o'clock most nights and they got back to the take-out just as the river water receded to its dammed flow rate. They dragged their gear to the designated drop-off area, changed out of their wet suits and sat on the river bank, dangling their feet in the clear cold water for a few minutes while they snacked on Paul's crackers and split the last coke. The staff dining room had closed at seven. They could have bought snacks at the store but he didn't want to face his fellow employees with the taste of Dahlia fresh on his lips.

They hitched a ride to staff housing by hanging out near the bridge. It was fully dark when they were dropped off. Paul kissed her lightly on the lips and they went off to their separate buildings to sleep and dream about paradise.

The Caverns Outdoor Center, COC, had grown from humble beginnings over its quarter-century existence. The heart of the business was located on an eighty-acre parcel of land in the Chattahoochee National Forest where Georgia Route 72, the Appalachian Trail and the Clancy River cross paths.

Despite its distance from any city, rafting, restaurants and boat rentals served thousands of people every day during the season from April through November. Many customers came from Atlanta. The Motel, the Restaurants, the Outfitter Store, the Instruction Department, and Guided Travel departments each generated substantial revenue, but the guided raft trips down five nearby rivers were the biggest moneymaker.

The mountain elevation here kept the nights cool and the days mild. The woodlands were beautiful now; they had recovered from destructive clear cutting that previous generations had wrought. Rivers and streams abounded. None were more beautiful than the Clancy River.

Paul Hunter was a pain is the ass so far as Cornelia K. Johnson was concerned. She ran the restaurant operation. She managed it, and had created it from scrub pine, sweat, and wisps of her dreams. So Paul had to go. God damn it! She liked him, but the staff, including cooks and shift managers were complaining about him.

"He stinks like a dog," Archie, the restaurant G.M. told her.

"Paul even looks dirty, and he refuses to follow the rules," the breakfast manager whispered.

"Which rules?" Cornelia asked. She was surprised because Paul was always polite.

"He won't give customers water when they're first seated. He insists on asking them if they'd like something to drink... they only get ice if they ask for it. Paul says it's better for the planet to conserve water.

"Then there's that crap about aluminum pans poisoning us. It's something about light metals causing Alzheimer's and memory loss. He won't recite the specials if they're cooked in aluminum pots."

"But all our pots are aluminum!" said Corney.

"Exactly," said the manager. "And I can't budge him. He talks about this stuff at shift meetings. I either look weak or the servers begin to grumble. They may be joking to tease either Paul or me. The situation gets worse every day."

Corney thought back to other conversations over the last months. Complaints from the kitchen might have been motivated by jealousy over Paul transferring from line cook to server. Some cooks tended to look down on people whose *only job* was to deliver the beautiful food they created in the hot and confused kitchen. Paul was a traitor. The head chef had warned her that Paul was too generous with salads and bread and that he seldom served a dessert.

"Corney, you got to shape him up. He's costing us money."

She nodded. Paul Hunter had to go.

If you'd like to share more of Paul's adventures, visit billserle.com

www.ingramcontent.com/pod-product-compliance
Lightning Source LLC
LaVergne TN
LVHW050615100826
845148LV00011B/1599

* 9 7 8 0 6 1 5 7 9 1 3 4 0 *